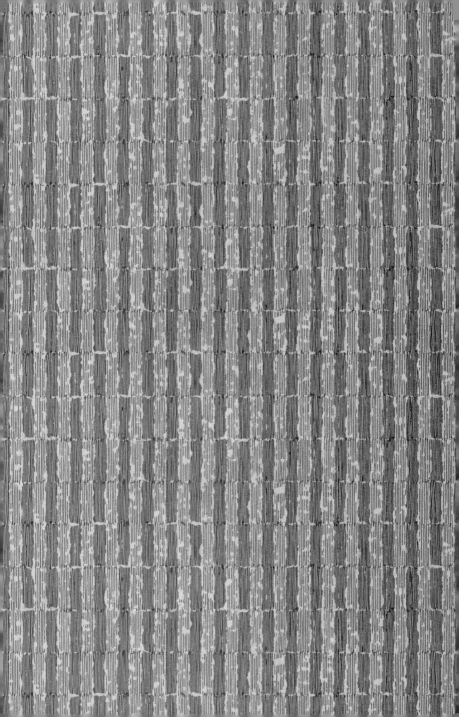

If ever in your life you are faced
with a choice, a difficult decision,
a quandary,

Ask yourself,
"What would Edgar and Ellen do?"

And do exactly the contrary.

Edgar & Ellen

TOURIST TRAP

Edgar & Ellen

TOURIST TRAP

by
CHARLES OGDEN

illustrations by
RICK CARTON

ALADDIN
NEW YORK   LONDON   TORONTO   SYDNEY

Watch out for Edgar & Ellen in:

Rare Beasts
Under Town
Pet's Revenge

❧ ALADDIN
An imprint of Simon & Schuster Children's Publishing Division
1230 Avenue of the Americas, New York, NY 10020
Text and illustrations copyright © 2004 by Star Farm Productions, LLC.

ALADDIN and colophon are trademarks of Simon & Schuster, Inc.

Designed by Star Farm Productions, LLC.
The text of this book was set in Bembo, Auldroon, P22 Typewriter, Brighton, and Cheltenham.
The illustrations in this book were rendered in pen and ink and digitally enhanced in Photoshop.
Manufactured in the United States of America
First Aladdin edition January 2006
10   9   8   7   6   5   4   3   2   1

Library of Congress Cataloging-in-Publication Data
Ogden, Charles.
Tourist trap / by Charles Ogden.
p. cm. — (Edgar & Ellen ; 2)
Summary: Devious twins Edgar and Ellen scheme to thwart the mayor's tourism initiative, which, if successful, would destroy the town junkyard, the twins' favorite playground, foraging spot, and home to their beloved carnivorous plant, Berenice. [1. Tourism—Fiction. 2. Twins—Fiction. 3. Brothers and sisters—Fiction. 4. Humorous stories.] I. Carton, Rick, ill. II. Title.
PZ7.O333 To 2004
[Fic]—dc22
2003018327
ISBN-13: 978-1-4169-1411-2
ISBN-10: 1-4169-1411-0

FOR THOSE WHO DARE TREAD NEAR...

Revenge Is Sweet

"Happy birthday to you! Happy birthday to you!"

Ellen covered her ears. She hated the "Happy Birthday" song. More than that, she hated the birthday girl.

Her lavender dress.

Her lilac patent-leather shoes.

The purple ribbons in her hair.

"I'm going to be sick, Brother," Ellen moaned, slumping against the wall.

"You don't want to miss the fireworks, do you?" Edgar asked. He peered out from behind the drapes that hid him and his sister from the party.

Ellen's eyes narrowed as she looked down at her left pinkie, which was missing its fingernail—lost in an incident involving the head of Stephanie Knightleigh's favorite doll and a claw hammer. Stephanie got a new doll. Ellen's fingernail had not grown back.

But when Ellen looked at the empty box crumpled in her *right* hand, she smiled.

The cook ushered an ornately decorated cake into the room, much to the excitement of the many singing guests. Thirteen fizzing candles sparked and crackled atop the tallest tier. Standing at the head of the table, the birthday girl nodded approvingly as the cook set the purple cake before her.

"Happy birthday, dear Stephanie...."

Edgar clutched at the drapes, drawing them to his mouth so the heavy fabric muffled his giggles. Ellen twisted a pigtail with her scarred finger.

Stephanie took a deep breath and leaned in.

Ex-ploosh!

Frosting erupted in all directions, and sugared rosebuds shot across the room like tiny cannonballs. Too late, the horrified partygoers threw their hands up to protect themselves from the torrent of frosting. The cook screamed.

Stephanie stood at the head of the table, fudgey cake splattered across her party dress and thick icing dripping from her red ringlets. The birthday girl stared at the spot where her beautiful cake once sat, all color drained from her face.

In the madness following the explosion, Edgar and Ellen slipped from behind the drapes and out the front door.

1. A Waxy Build-Up

Years and years ago, when candles were just as important as lightbulbs are today, a man named Nod built a wax factory. Many people came to work at Nod's factory, and as it became the largest supplier of wax in the region and word of Nod's success spread, a settlement grew on the banks of the Running River. Thus the village of Nod's Limbs was born.

At first Nod's Limbs was no more than a collection of houses located upstream from the factory. After a long day, workers would retire to the local tavern, where they could enjoy a hot meal, spin a good yarn, and partake in friendly contests of strength and wit. As their families grew, so did their desire for a finer life, and the factory workers wanted a real town with a government that would provide them with everything hardworking citizens deserved.

Nod, however, had no interest in running a town; he wanted to run his factory. To him, the workers' lives seemed small and dreary. He paid their wages, and paid them well, and that was that. However, another more popular man was eager to helm the budding township, and so the people elected Thaddeus Knightleigh, the sociable tavern owner, as the first mayor of Nod's Limbs. This proved a fateful choice, because a Knightleigh has served as mayor ever since.

This original Mayor Knightleigh ordered the construction of many notable buildings, such as a large town hall where citizens gathered to hear him speak, a theater where audiences enjoyed the entertainment of the day, a clock tower so everyone would always know the time, and seven covered bridges so people could cross the river that runs through the town. Thaddeus Knightleigh's wife, who descended from a family of French hatmakers, wanted to bring culture and sophistication to the rural community, so she organized plays and founded a dress shop that made clothes in the latest Parisian styles.

To his dismay, Thaddeus Knightleigh could never persuade the townspeople to rename Nod's Limbs "Knightleighville," because the citizens felt obliged to show some respect to the man who paid their salaries.

2. The Birth of the Wrong Side of Town

From these earliest days, the people of Nod's Limbs led simple and carefree lives, and if your life were as simple and carefree as the Nod's Limbsians', you would probably be just as chipper. Here smiles never wavered; no one cursed or quarreled or said a bad word about the weather, even when rain flooded cellars or snow heaped above windows.

How awfully pleasant.

The population expanded, and families thrived and babies were born, and, inevitably, people died from sickness or old age. So the time came for Nod's Limbs to build a cemetery. But Thaddeus Knightleigh did not want anything so gloomy to blemish his charming town.

At about that time, piles of rubbish turned from nuisance to eyesore, and the citizens clamored for a junkyard where they could discard items for which they no longer had any use. Thaddeus, who did not understand the purpose of scavenging something used when one could buy something new, felt the same way about junkyards as he did about cemeteries.

So, in a brilliant maneuver, he combined the two. A small section of the forest was cleared away far south of the town hall, the theater, and the clock tower, and this became the site of the Nod's Limbs Cemetery and Junkyard. Over many years, Nod's Limbs grew and neighborhoods sprouted up far beyond the center of town, but the area around the cemetery and junkyard remained deserted.

Well, almost deserted.

One narrow house rose impossibly high, towering over the junkyard and cemetery. Iron spikes jutted up from the roof of this pillar of gray stone, and the building itself seemed to suck all color from its surroundings. Two half-moon windows kept careful watch for the rare passerby, and just above, a round window in the cupola winked in and out of the heavy mist like a third eye. Cracked and broken gray shutters banged against their twisted frames at the slightest gust of wind, and carved above the dark entryway was the word *schadenfreude*, which means "pleasure derived from the misery of others." A fitting motto for the only two people who lived in the tall mansion: the young twins named Edgar and Ellen.

3. Lunchtime Schemes

Edgar and Ellen were avoiding the sun one lovely spring day. Edgar worked feverishly on a new idea in the game room, drawing out his plans atop a battered chessboard and tacking his finished work to the wall with rusty darts. Up in the kitchen, Ellen stood over a pot on the cast-iron stove. She fished a small jar from the depths of the spice rack and shook its contents into Edgar's bowl of porridge.

She grabbed a tin can suspended from a garden hose over the washbasin and called into it, "*Brother! Lunch is ready!*"

Her voice echoed through the hose and rang out of another tin can hanging in the game room.

Edgar had secretly constructed this makeshift intercom the year before by lacing a series of hoses and cans throughout the house's thirteen floors. One night when Ellen thought he was outside extinguishing fireflies, Edgar spoke to her through the intercom, pretending that his rumbling, disembodied voice was that of a distant uncle who died of the plague. Although unnerved at first, Ellen soon realized her rare opportunity to learn about the afterlife. She assaulted her uncle with questions until his answers betrayed the hoax—"There are no sisters here" was a dead giveaway—and she locked her brother in the subbasement for two hours.

"I'm coming. I'm *coming*." Edgar's voice rang in the kitchen. He gathered his papers and took them upstairs to the adjoining dining room where Ellen sat eating her porridge.

"As you can see, Sister, these are the initial plans for Operation: Whiplash."

Ellen examined the sketch of a giant fan aimed at skaters at the Roly-Poly Rainbo Roller Rink. In Edgar's drawing a number of skaters whirled into one another and against the walls of the rink. Edgar had painstakingly drawn the resulting cuts and bruises.

"It'll be like bumper cars— *Bump! Thump! Fahwump!* Then no one will ever return, and we'll have the roller rink all to ourselves. We have that turbine engine down in the basement—all we need are objects to use as fan blades," said Edgar, gazing at the plans as he swallowed a spoonful of porridge.

A painful, prickling sensation spread down his skinny throat, as if he were being stung by a hundred baby hornets, and he immediately started to choke. With watering eyes, he looked up to see Ellen grinning at him and holding a jar labeled STINGING NETTLES. It was empty save for a few needlelike thorns at the bottom.

Edgar ran coughing and hacking to the kitchen for a glass of water.

Ellen strolled over to the window.

"Fan blades...fan blades. Well, then, we must pay a visit next door."

She gazed down on the tombstones overgrown with weeds and blackened by years of exposure. Her eyes moved over the low slate wall at the back of the cemetery to the enormous trash heap just beyond.

"Ah, how lucky we are to have such a beautiful view," she sighed, as her brother crept up behind her, his hands cradling a rotten egg.

4. The Gadget Graveyard

After Ellen scraped the reeking slime from her hair, she and Edgar trooped down several flights of stairs to their front door, the footies of their frayed pajamas *slap-slapping* against each step. The tall, scrawny twins hardly ever wore anything but the comfy outfits, and the original red-and-white stripes had long ago faded to a dirty rust and gray.

They emerged, squinting, from the gloom of the front hall, their greasy black hair gleaming in the sun. Slinking across their yard and into the cemetery, they skirted the back row of gravestones—IN MEMORY OF BERTEL HERRINGBOTTLE, DIED FROM AN INFESTATION OF THE CUCKOO WASP, 1823 was one of the twins' particular favorites—and vanished into the depths of the junkyard.

At first the inhabitants of Nod's Limbs used the junkyard as a kind of secondhand store. They disposed of old mixing bowls, wooden spoons, dulled hatchets, and empty ink bottles, and maybe found a spinning wheel in usable condition to take home. But as the years passed, more and more garbage piled up, and fewer people came to forage through it, until the junkyard became a sprawl of rusty bicycles, worn

rubber tires, defunct transistor radios, chipped flower-pots, and other abandoned rubbish.

So much broken glass and sharp metal was strewn about that mothers forbade their children to go near the place, and a former mayor posted DANGER and WARNING signs at the junkyard's entrance.

But no one forbade Edgar and Ellen to go near it, for their parents were away, traveling on an around-the-world holiday, according to the note they'd left behind years earlier. The twins considered the items in the junkyard neither useless nor dangerous, or rather, not dangerous to *them*. Their attic was filled with articles they had discovered there over the years, a collection upon which they depended for inspiration. Edgar had found the equipment for the intercom system there, and he always carried a large, ratty satchel filled with junkyard loot for use in emergencies. The twins even affectionately renamed the place the "Gadget Graveyard."

Edgar clambered up the heaps of debris, teetering for a moment at the top of each before skidding to the ground. Meanwhile, Ellen hurled bolts and rivets at her brother as she picked her way to the back of the junkyard. There, nestled in the crook of an old bed frame, an enormous plant soaked up the sun.

5. Berenice

"Hello, Berenice," said Ellen. "Let's see what's in your lunch box today."

Berenice was another reason the twins cherished the Gadget Graveyard. Ellen discovered her when she was just a sprout topped with small, pink swellings that looked like lips, and she had been delighted to see the plant suck a circling fly into her gullet. For years she had tried to raise carnivorous species in her own garden, but the plants refused to thrive in Nod's Limbs' climate. How one came to grow in the junkyard, Ellen could never explain, but she took it upon herself to care for Berenice and built an insect trap by lining an old pail with sticky paper.

Berenice turned out to be a particularly hungry carnivore, and feeding her became one of the twins' greatest pleasures. Even Edgar, who had never had much of a green thumb, loved providing the plant with flies, beetles, small spiders, and any other insects he could find.

Ellen retrieved the pail and plucked the victims one by one from the gluey paper, gently placing them on Berenice's bulbous lips. Berenice's throat hissed and crackled like frying bacon as she digested the bugs. Ellen had to be careful, however. Hard white seeds lined Berenice's mouth, giving the plant a toothy smile. Once Edgar stuck his finger between her jaws, and it took the twins' combined strength to pry them open again. Edgar still had the scar from where one of the seeds had pierced his index finger.

Ellen looked at all the withered seedpods littering the ground beneath the bed frame. Every evening the kernels fell from the plant's mouth, leaving Berenice toothless, and every morning new ones had sprung up in their place. It was just another one of Berenice's mysteries.

"I don't get it, Brother," Ellen said. "I've planted tons of Berenice's seeds, and none of them have sprouted. Maybe she's not getting enough nutrients."

"Not likely, with you gorging her every day," Edgar called out from behind a washing machine. "Are you going to *burp* her too? Leave off the plant and get to work!"

Ellen threw a nicked paperweight in Edgar's direction and started digging among the scraps, foraging for potential giant fan blades. She showed him an old car door, but Edgar dismissed it as too heavy.

They checked under ruptured pipes and on top of rickety scaffolding, from pile to pile across the junkyard, and while they searched, the twins sang:

> *Behind the graves of men deceased*
> *Lie piles of refuse, grimed with grease.*
> *Forsaken rubbish rests in peace*
> *Until we raid the gadget feast.*
> *Tarnished chalkboards, copper spoons,*
> *Wrinkly, crinkly, rotting prunes,*
> *A pool cue makes a great harpoon—*
> *Oh, what a lovely afternoon!*
> *A treasure trove of pranks to play—*
> *Who'd go and toss this stuff away?*

"How about this surfboard?" Ellen asked.

"Hmmm...maybe," Edgar replied.

He was mulling over her discovery when the twins heard voices from over the cemetery wall.

6. An Alarming Intrusion

"A funeral!" Ellen whispered to her brother. But the voices approached the Gadget Graveyard, and the twins ducked behind a tower of discarded tractor tires.

Edgar and Ellen rarely saw anyone near the junkyard. They peeked out from behind the tires, and to their surprise, saw Mayor Knightleigh standing at the dump's entrance.

His navy suit barely contained the belly that ballooned out over his wide belt. At his side, dwarfed by her father, was his eldest child, Stephanie.

"What is *she* doing here?" Ellen said through clenched teeth, tugging at Edgar's ear.

"OW! I see, I *see*! Let go!" Edgar swatted at her hand.

Mayor Knightleigh surveyed the expanse of trash, and as he stooped to unlock his leather briefcase, a button popped off his shirt. He failed to notice. He opened an overstuffed notebook and jotted down a few words.

"Where's Miles?" he demanded.

"I'm not my brother's keeper, Daddy," Stephanie replied, but she nonetheless turned back toward the cemetery and called, "Miles! *Miles*, get in here."

A young boy, small for his nine years, with freckles and sandy hair falling in his face, ran in carrying a pad of paper and some crayons.

"Stephie! Look! I made a grave rubbing!" Miles said proudly. He held up an image of a skull with the words HERE LIES NATHANIEL FORTESQUE; DON'T DO WHAT HE DID OR YOU'LL LOSE YOUR HEAD TOO etched underneath.

"Miles, you are *so* morbid," Stephanie said. "Just stay out of trouble and don't get dirty."

Miles gave her a thumbs-up and ran off again. Stephanie pulled out a camera and snapped a few pictures while her father wrote in his notebook. She paused a moment, crinkling her nose at the lingering scent of decay, and smoothed the skirt of her lilac dress.

Ellen frowned. She hated pastels in principle, and Stephanie wore some light shade of purple every day. She felt compelled to lob a ball of dirt at Stephanie when a gleeful squeal from the back of the junkyard made her freeze midthrow.

"Wow! What kind of a plant is *this*?"

Miles had wandered into the bowels of the dump and stumbled on the rusty bed frame where Berenice reclined. He reached down to touch the pink lips. Berenice waited expectantly. So did the twins.

"Hope he doesn't want that finger!" said Edgar. He grinned and cracked his knuckles.

"*Miles!* What are you doing?" Stephanie yelled, spying him through the viewfinder of her camera. She hurried over, grabbed her brother's outstretched hand, and only then got a good look at what had so enthralled him.

"*Ew!* Why would you want to touch that thing?"

"It's neat," Miles said quietly. He kept his eyes on the ground as Stephanie dragged him back to their father.

The twins sighed in disappointment.

Berenice snapped up a moth.

"All right, Stephanie," the mayor said, scribbling some final notes. "This will do just fine. You took the photos?"

"Yes, Daddy," the girl replied. "Let's get out of here. This place is gross."

"Oh, it won't be for long, my dear. Not for long." The mayor opened his briefcase and shoved his notebook inside. A single stray page floated to the ground, but none of the Knightleighs noticed.

"Dad," Miles said, "what are you going to do with this place?"

"Why, beautify it, my boy. Make it useful." The mayor folded his hands over his belly as he gazed over the mounds of refuse. "And my plans will do something my great-great-great-great-great-great-great-granddaddy Thaddeus never could: make the name of Knightleigh more famous than the name of Nod."

Miles kicked at the dirt. "But you won't get rid of that plant, will you?" he asked.

"Of course, Miles! This plant, that plant—they'll go the way of all this junk. The grubby weeds in this mess don't have a place in my designs, not if I can help it, and I'm the mayor, so I *can* help it!"

Stephanie nodded, but Miles kept staring at the ground.

"But, Dad—," he started.

"Miles, that's enough! I don't want to hear any more about it." Mayor Knightleigh took his son by the arm. "Come on. I'm very busy and can't hang about here all day."

He and Stephanie marched out of the junkyard, dragging Miles along behind them. As they disappeared into the cemetery, the twins emerged from their hiding spot.

"Ellen," Edgar asked, "what was all that about? What could the Knightleighs possibly want with our Gadget Graveyard?"

"That Stephanie—what does *she* know about plants? I swear to you, the next time I see her, I will make her eat one of those ringlets...," Ellen said.

"Why would they take pictures? And what did Knightleigh mean by *'they'll go the way of all this junk'*? What is he planning?"

"...And I'm going to shred those stupid ribbons!"

"Ellen! Quit worrying about Stephanie!" Edgar yanked one of Ellen's pigtails. "We've got to figure out what the mayor is up to!"

Ellen turned to face her brother. "How *dare* they threaten Berenice," she said. "Grubby weed, *indeed*. She's one of the most handsome plants on the planet. What do you have in mind, Brother?"

Edgar didn't answer. He picked up the mayor's lost page and quickly scanned it, letting out a hard, short laugh before handing it to Ellen.

"Alas, Operation: Whiplash will have to wait, Sister. Look!"

Under the official seal of the mayor's office, the
flier read:

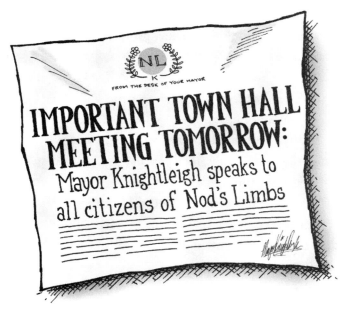

7. Breaking and Entering

At noon the next day, the twins were crawling
through a dark, cramped air shaft.

"Ow. Quit pushing."

"Well, move faster! Where's his office?"

Edgar wore a miner's helmet with a lamp to light their way. He paused to examine a blueprint of Town Hall. The twins had entered the ventilation system through an exhaust duct on the roof. Navigating the narrow vent shafts was grim and dirty work. It suited the twins well.

"We're close. It should be up here on the left," he said.

"Hurry up!" said Ellen. "We've got to get in and out before he finishes."

"Well, then, we have all day, don't we? That windbag loves to hear himself talk." Edgar inched around a corner and stopped in front of a grate right above the mayor's desk. Ellen smacked into him.

"Careful!" he said, checking the blueprint again. "Okay. This should be it." He pulled a screwdriver out of his satchel and unscrewed the grate cover. It fell to the floor with a *clang*.

"*Shhh!*" hissed Ellen.

"What are you so worried about?" Edgar said. "Everyone in town is outside for the speech." The twins dropped into the mayor's office. Through an open window, they heard the murmur of the crowd and the whistle of a microphone being set in place.

They scanned the spacious room. A large oak desk stood in the center, with a nameplate that read MAYOR KNIGHTLEIGH, HONORED AND ESTIMABLE HEAD HONCHO. Two paintings hung on opposite sides of the office, facing each other. One was of Mayor Knightleigh and the other was a portrait of the Emperor Napoleon. However, on closer inspection, Edgar realized the second painting was actually Mayor Knightleigh dressed up as Napoleon.

Bookshelves lined the walls, filled with brightly polished trophies and awards inscribed with Mayor Knightleigh's name. On the wall behind the desk hung a large map of Nod's Limbs. Several purple pushpins called out landmarks around Nod's Limbs, such as the clock tower and the Museum of Wax.

"What are all these pins for?" asked Edgar.

"What's *this* one?" asked Ellen. Next door to their property at the edge of town, in the plot labeled CEMETERY & JUNKYARD, a large red pushpin stuck out from the map.

"I've got a feeling this blowhard mayor is up to no good," said Edgar.

"I agree," said Ellen. "We must be able to find a clue here somewhere."

A small filing cabinet stood in one corner of the office, and Ellen attacked this first, jimmying the lock with a skate key from Edgar's satchel. Edgar sifted through a stack of papers on the mayor's desk. They heard one more blast of feedback, and then the mayor's voice echoed from outside:

"Welcome, my fellow Nod's Limbsians! In light of my many accomplishments as mayor of this fine town and the success of my unopposed campaigns for three terms running, I requested your presence here today on the steps of our town hall to announce a major announcement. I have planned yet another program of extraordinary proportion and great ambition for Nod's Limbs, which will provide even more benefits to our town than last year's tremendously successful mayoral initiatives. It will pump much-needed funds into our local economy, add building projects and jobs, and increase our pride in this historically important, yet forward-looking community. This program will put Nod's Limbs on the map!"

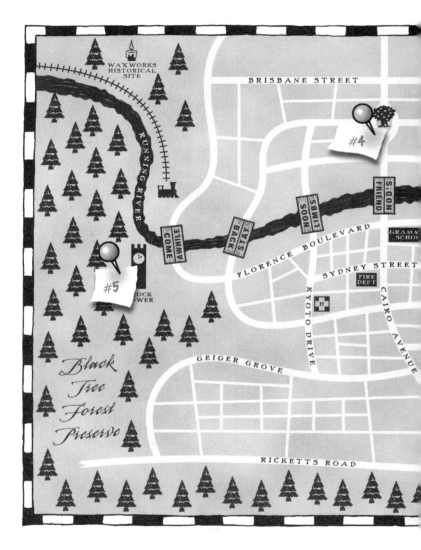

Ellen wrenched open the cabinet drawer and groaned. "It's going to take forever to go through all these!" She fingered row after row of hanging files.

Outside the mayor continued:

> "What, you are most certainly asking your-selves, is this exceptional and phenomenally exciting program for our beloved town? Well, stop asking, because you don't have the answer. I, Mayor Knightleigh, have the answer!
>
> "I am staging a series of thrilling festivals and parades celebrating the cultured practices of our town. Because if Nod's Limbs has one thing in abundance, it's culture and sophistica-tion, dating all the way back to our very first esteemed mayor, Thaddeus Knightleigh."

"I don't know if a wax museum counts as culture and sophistication," said Edgar as he scanned the papers. He didn't find any mention of the junkyard, but a manila folder caught his attention.

Scrawled across the top was the title VIP TOUR, and beneath that, stamped in bright red letters, CONFI-DENTIAL. Edgar quickly opened the file and read the following:

CONFIDENTIAL MEMORANDUM

TO: Mayor Knightleigh, Head Honcho
FROM: Staff Committee on Tourism
         Initiative

Summarized below is our background research on the people invited for the tour and festival. These VIPs fit the profiles you requested. The support of these individuals should convince the National Registry of Historic Treasures to approve our application, which will surely make your project a success.

"'Surely make your project a success'?" echoed Edgar. "He's inviting people here for a tour? Why would a Very Important Person want to come *here*?" He continued reading:

NILS AND NORA DE GROOT

Husband-and-wife architect team. The number one name in design—thirty years ago. Currently the thirty-eighth name (names one through thirty-seven were busy or didn't respond to your invitation). Past projects include a school playground in Iceland made from durable wicker, and a floating phone booth for oil rigs in the Gulf of Thailand. Hope next job will return them to limelight. Are willing to work with your design ideas. Have requested that all pictures in their hotel room be covered in cheesecloth because "it frees our brains from the shackles of the mundane."

BLAKE GLIDE

Action hero of the silver screen. Starred in such movies as "Mr. Destruction" and "Fatal Bludgeon" 1 through 9. His one attempt at Shakespeare, "RoboHamlet," flopped. In recent years, has wanted to perform "serious works with non-exploding content." Seeks to invest in a hotel, restaurant, or resort featuring dinner theater where he can be the regular headliner. Rumored involvement with many leading ladies, but not currently attached. Press bio lists hobbies as hang gliding, sky boarding, defying death.

MARY FEEMORE

Freelance writer for a B-list travel brochure company. Sent a letter to your office requesting a spot on the tour. Willing to pay her own way. No background info available.

ALEX SAI

Award-winning travel journalist and chief travel editor at the "Capital Times." Nationally syndicated column appears in all magazines that matter. No spouse, children, or pets. Based in New York City, but keeps apartments in London and Rio de Janeiro. Exceedingly influential, considered the last word on which destinations are hot and which are not. Known espresso addict.

Edgar set the folder back on the desk. "Curious," he muttered.

Outside, the mayor droned on:

> *"Tourists will come for breathtaking cavalcades and informative tours of our charming city. To this end, I have planned an inaugural tour of Nod's Limbs for invited VIPs and celebrities, whose support will surely convince the National Registry of Historic Treasures to approve our application for historic-treasure status. It's high time the world experienced Nod's Limbs."*

Ellen continued leafing through the files alphabetically. "Jailbreaks, Jumbotrons," she read.

"...and for a stupendous opening, I—I mean, we—will kick off with... ahem... a nod to the Knightleigh family's French ancestry, the ancestry that helped build our great town: the Nod's Limbs' First Annual French Toast Festival, which will feature a cook-off, a parade, and the unveiling of my top-secret surprise!"

The twins could hear *oohs* and *aahs* coming from the crowd.

"So, celebrity tourists are coming to Nod's Limbs. I still don't understand how Knightleigh swindled them into visiting this town. The Hotel Motel is the only place to stay, and it's rattier than Heimertz's shed!" Edgar said.

Heimertz was the caretaker of the twins' house and grounds, and while neither of them had ever seen the inside of his shed, the exterior hardly seemed hospitable.

"AHA!" shouted Ellen.

She pulled a file titled JUNKYARD RECONSTRUCTION PLANS from the cabinet and removed glossy renderings of an even glossier building from the folder.

Ellen gasped.

The images were of a tall building with two half-moon windows and a cupola. A row of Nod's Limbs' flags lined the roof, and all the windows had sparkling clean, white shutters. Violet rose bushes bordered the spotless green lawn, and the building was painted powdery-pastel lavender.

Edgar came to look. "It looks like *our* house, Ellen... but in some kind of nightmare." He had never seen anything so terrifying.

"I think this is what the whole tourism program is about, Edgar." Ellen pointed to the title block at the bottom of a drawing, which read THE KNIGHT-LORIAN HOTEL, ON FORMER JUNKYARD SITE.

"Knightleigh wants to build his own fancy hotel on top of the Gadget Graveyard, and he needs guests to fill the rooms!"

"He can't do that! It's ours!" said Edgar. "We'll lose our supplies. Do you realize the plans I have?"

"Look!" wailed Ellen. "Cupid fountains on the front lawn. And are those...those aren't...daisies? Disgusting!"

The thought of the cheerful flowers chilled Ellen and reminded her of something else.

"Edgar," she said, "they'll kill Berenice."

The twins stared at the papers before them, then at each other.

> *"We will give the very first tour one week from today, on the morning of the French Toast Festival. As for the official Nod's Limbs Tour Guide, I have appointed a worthy scholar, Miss Stephanie Knightleigh, who recently received an A+ on her history paper titled 'The Unabridged History of Nod's Limbs.'"*

Stephanie Knightleigh's name jolted Ellen out of her stupor. She strode to the window and scowled at Stephanie, who stood in a lavender suit near her father, bowing dramatically. Amid a smattering of polite applause, the mayor smiled proudly.

> *"This initiative is the product of my many months and long hours of thinking, pondering, and contemplating. I ask you, the honorable citizens of Nod's Limbs, to join me in my self-less quest to bring our town the international acclaim and overwhelming fame and fortune I deserve—I mean, it deserves."*

8. Tossing Some Ideas Around

Edgar and Ellen were shadowy spots in the bright sunlight as they trudged home in silence. Turning from Ricketts Road onto the nameless lane that led to their house, the twins cringed when they caught sight of their beloved junkyard.

They plodded through the front door of their home into the murky hallway and started up the stairs. On each landing they passed one item after another recovered from the Gadget Graveyard: a collection of dusty glass eyes, the remains of a yellowed wedding dress that Ellen wore to scare small children, and an oil lantern the twins used when exploring the sewers. They finally reached the fourth-floor study, where Pet lounged on a tattered sofa.

Edgar and Ellen found Pet years ago in the sub-basement and decided to keep the small, limbless bundle of matted hair. Pet's only distinct feature was its single yellowish eye that stared out atop the hairy heap. Pet was far too slow to slink away unnoticed, and Edgar grabbed it by its filthy scruff and scrunched it up.

"Knightleigh is going to destroy the Gadget Graveyard, Sister. He's going to uproot Berenice and cart her away to some...*trash dump*," he said, winding up his pitching arm. Ellen waited for the throw. The twins often played their own version of catch when they had something on their minds; Pet was their favorite ball.

Fwump.

Pet landed in Ellen's outstretched hands. "The mayor said the maiden tour is next week. There's no way he can build his hotel by then."

Pet's milky yellow eyeball wandered back and forth, visible only through the narrow gaps between Ellen's fingers. Ellen turned her back toward Edgar and swung Pet through her legs. Pet spun through the air like a shaggy yo-yo.

Whoomp.

Edgar caught Pet with one hand. "True," he said,

and a gleam shone in his eye. "And he can only build his hotel if lots of tourists *want* to visit. That's why he needs those celebrities to come—those famous architects will build the hotel, the actor will pay for it, and the journalists will tell people to vacation in Nod's Limbs!" Edgar tossed Pet back to Ellen, purposely throwing it too short.

"So," Ellen said, diving for the ball of hair and skinning her knees on the carpet, "we just need to stop them. But I don't know why Knightleigh thinks someone would designate Nod's Limbs a national historic treasure," she added, juggling Pet one-handed."

"And what about that 'worthy scholar'?" asked Edgar, puffing out his belly in imitation of the mayor. "Stephanie Knightleigh is giving the tour."

Ellen raised an eyebrow. "It would be a pity if Stephanie arrived too late." She stepped into her pitch and aimed Pet right at Edgar's forehead.

Thwack.

"Wouldn't it, Brother?" she asked.

"Indeed, Sister, that would be most unfortunate," Edgar said, rubbing his head. "Alas, who would lead those poor tourists then?"

"Those poor tourists who are supposed to love our charming community? What if they *didn't*? What if they never wanted to come back, ever again?" asked Ellen.

"There would be no need for a new hotel," Edgar said.

"And no need to clear the junkyard—or uproot Berenice," finished Ellen.

Pet, who had bounced off Edgar's forehead onto the floor, shuffled under the sofa as the twins left the room.

9. Culture and Sophistication

Meanwhile, the rest of Nod's Limbs was getting ready for the visitors' arrival and the French Toast Festival by turning their town into the center of urban refinement they always thought it might be.

Inspired by the royal gardens of Versailles, and armed with new clippers courtesy of the mayor's hedge fund, Mr. Poshi planned an elaborate design for the shrubbery in front of his house. Next door, Mrs. Jackson was doing some trimming of her own. She clipped away at her dog, Roxy, trying to model the basset hound's coat after the fashion of a French poodle. Roxy was not enjoying the experience.

Throughout the town, people mowed their lawns,

repainted their houses with brighter, happier colors, and planted flowers along the sidewalks. Downtown, store owners swept their entryways and restocked their shelves. Mr. Barbarino, the proprietor of one of Nod's Limbs' busiest restaurants, added French toast to his lunch and dinner menus, and Miss Gomez displayed pictures of fancy European hairstyles in her salon.

The goings-on around Town Hall especially fascinated everyone. Surrounding a large area to the left of the building, a vast covered fence, several stories tall, had been erected. TOP SECRET and KEEP OUT signs hung all over it, and the town could hear construction workers, machinery, and various clangings and bangings from behind the barricade at all hours.

Whatever was hidden behind that fence, it was *big,* and the mayor took care to keep his nosy citizens uninformed.

10. On the Map

The twins stayed in the library most of the week. Not the Nod's Limbs Public Library, but their very own library, which took up the entire eighth floor of their house. Edgar and Ellen found the room very useful: the library held excellent hiding places for their treacherous games of hide-and-seek, and the soot from its fireplace was ideal for leaving handprints on cars, houses, and windows around the neighborhood.

The books in the library, however, were a different matter. Aside from the copy of *War and Peace* that Ellen liked to drop on Edgar's toes from time to time, most of the musty volumes stood untouched.

Brother and sister sat side by side at a giant mahogany desk, surrounded by stacks of books. Edgar had swiped the tour schedule from the mayor's office, so they knew exactly when and where Stephanie planned to take the celebrities, but the twins had their own ideas about how to make those sites memorable.

Next to Ellen sat *The Landmarks and History of Nod's Limbs* and *Nod's Limbs Fun Facts*, and as she flipped through their pages, she couldn't believe someone had taken the time to write them. In another stack sat much more interesting books, such as Mary Shelley's *Frankenstein*, Bram Stoker's *Dracula*, and *The Gruesome Guide to Gory Movies.*

Directly in front of Edgar was a rusted Underwood Standard typewriter, black with gold lettering, which had surfaced on a particularly rewarding trip to the Gadget Graveyard. As Edgar typed, Ellen read aloud

descriptions of Nod's Limbs landmarks, peppering the guidebook entries with ideas inspired by the works of the other authors. She then traced illustrations from books about monsters, vampires, and other creatures of the night and pasted her drawings next to the new text.

Ellen leaned over, supervising Edgar's work. "You spelled 'buccaneer' wrong. It has only one *n*."

"It's your fault for giving me such a difficult word. I keep having to start over—there's no Back button on this typewriter!"

"This has to look professional. I'm not going out there with a shoddy guidebook, so keep typing until it's right." Ellen swiveled back to her books, poring over some remarkably vivid pictures of skeletons.

When they were both satisfied with their work, Ellen bound the pages together and created a cover for the book, which she titled *Don't Go: Nod's Limbs.*

11. They're Here

With all these preparations, the week passed quickly. The day before the festival was scheduled to begin, Mayor Knightleigh waited in front of the Hotel

Motel, anxiously tugging at the cuffs of his jacket and straightening his tie. Stephanie stood at the lobby entrance behind him holding a plate of fresh croissants, compliments of Buffy's Muffins (which was now called Buffy's Patisserie in the spirit of culture and sophistication). A small crowd bustled about the parking lot, and seven townspeople held signs spelling out a friendly message, identical to one of the greetings painted across the town's seven covered bridges: WELCOME FRIEND TO NOD'S LIMBS STAY AWHILE.

With a screech of brakes and a diesel shudder, a sleek bus pulled up to the hotel. At the mayor's cue, the hospitality committee began to cheer and wave.

The bus door opened and Nils de Groot slipped down the stairs and into the sunlight with long, fluid steps. He wore a black suit with a black turtleneck, and his silver hair fell across his shoulders like wisps of smoke. The renowned architect spread his arms wide and strode past the mayor's waiting handshake.

"I'm having a vision," he cried, gazing at the shabby hotel. "It's as clear as a dewdrop on a calla lily: this is where the village of Lob's Limbs must build an upside-down sundial. Made of solid nickel! It shall be your finest achievement."

"No, no, Nils!" Nora de Groot stood at the bus's top step, feet planted widely apart and white-gloved hands perched on her hips. "Can't you see it, Nils? The clarity of the light, the pitch of the hills, these humble structures—this village positively cries out for a bell-shaped firehouse! Made of carved alabaster and decorated with black paint spots." As she spoke, she flitted from the bus, her billowy white dress and head scarf fluttering behind her.

The architects swept into the hotel in animated disagreement, ignoring the mayor.

"*Nod's* Limbs is officially larger than a village," Mayor Knightleigh called after them. "We're a town."

Following the de Groots off the bus, Mary Feemore, a petite young woman, clutched a yellow notepad. The mayor had been told that she wrote for a small company that placed travel brochures at highway rest stops, but he neither read travel brochures nor visited highway rest stops. At least her company had paid for her trip; the mayor's office was personally funding the tour for the rest of the VIPs, and between travel and lodging costs, it was quite expensive.

Mary Feemore looked tired, but her face brightened when she saw the mayor and Stephanie.

"Hello, Mr. Mayor. Allow me to introduce myself,"

she said, grabbing his still-extended hand for a friendly shake.

"Yes, it is lovely weather, isn't it?" he said, looking over Mary's shoulder and brushing her aside.

The mayor focused on the next figure in the doorway, and he wasn't the only one: the welcoming crowd started shouting and pointing and jostling for a better look. It was Blake Glide, the famous Hollywood leading man. The star of thirty-some blockbuster action films paused at the top step and cocked his head, allowing any nearby photographers the clearest shot of his unmistakable profile. He doffed his cap and ran his fingers through his stylishly messy hair, flashing a bright smile.

After acknowledging the mayor with a warm greeting, Blake Glide sauntered over to the swarm of fans and curious onlookers. He shook hands and repeatedly gave the thumbs-up sign, until a pasty girl with a pointy chin and blond wig elbowed her way to the front, shoving a pen and paper in Blake Glide's face.

"Can I have your autograph?" she asked.

"Anything for my number-one fan," he said with a wink. "What do you want it to say?"

" 'To Edgar: You stink like a rotting, bloated bird carcass.' "

Blake Glide started to write, but stopped abruptly.

"Ah. I see," he said, frowning slightly. "I'll just sign my name. How about that?"

"Whatever." The girl took the pen and the signed paper from him and said as she stalked away, "Thank you so very much. I've always wanted a bus driver's autograph."

The adoring public continued to clamor for Blake Glide's attention, leaving the mayor alone to greet the most influential VIP of all.

"Let me be the first to welcome you to historic Nod's Limbs, Ms. Sai," he said as the last figure stepped out.

"Thanks *a lot*," Alex Sai snarled, descending to the pavement. "It's just thrilling to be in a town smaller than my apartment."

She wore rimless sunglasses tinted blue, a cell-phone earpiece in one ear, and a pen behind the other. She gave the mayor a dismissive glance and looked at the fresh-faced citizens of Nod's Limbs waving and clapping. She yawned.

Stephanie leaped into the awkward silence.

"Welcome to Nod's Limbs, Ms. Sai. Would you like a croissant?" she asked, shooting her father a concerned look.

"I don't eat processed flour and sugar," Alex Sai replied coolly.

"Of course; that must be how you keep your terrific figure," the mayor said, wearing his best campaign smile. "I don't like any process in my sugar either."

Alex Sai glanced at Knightleigh's round belly. "Riiight," she said.

"Nod's Limbs is a town of remarkable heritage and cultural traditions. We have a lot of wonderful things planned for you, Ms. Sai," said the mayor.

She looked over her sunglasses at the Hotel Motel. "Well, I hope one of those things is a double espresso."

12. Toolhardy

That night Edgar and Ellen met in their attic-above-the-attic to go over their checklist.

"Red paint."

"Check."

"Rope."

"Check."

"Wrench."

Ellen didn't answer; instead she turned to peer through the large telescope behind her. It was the only object in the attic-above-the-attic, and its positioning behind a hatch in the roof provided them with a brilliant view of all of Nod's Limbs. Even though it was getting very late, Ellen could see the townspeople busily preparing for tomorrow's parade and festival.

"*Wrench,*" Edgar repeated. Ellen still didn't respond. She kept her eye pressed against the lens, lowered the angle of the telescope, and looked straight down into their backyard until she saw what she needed: Heimertz's toolbox sat unattended just outside his shed.

"Wrench. Check. You just need to go and get it."

Edgar and Ellen felt something toward Heimertz that they didn't feel toward anyone else: dread. The caretaker, who never seemed to take care of anything, had an eerie habit of appearing out of thin air. They hated his stare, which seemed to pierce their very thoughts, and his Cheshire cat smile that never wavered. But Heimertz never condemned or commented on the twins' misdeeds. In fact, Heimertz had never spoken a word to them at all.

The thought of skulking around Heimertz's shed made Ellen shiver, but if that toolbox held a wrench, someone would have to steal it. Ellen stepped away from the telescope to allow Edgar to see for himself.

"Are you crazy?" he shouted. "For all we know, he may be sleeping in his shed *right this second*!"

"More reason for you to go now," Ellen replied calmly.

"Me! Why me?"

"You're the Houdini," she said, raising her voice. Edgar enjoyed practicing the techniques of the world's greatest escape artists, and his abilities had come in handy many times.

"That's true," he said. "I am a master." Still, he hesitated a moment before tiptoeing down flight upon flight of winding steps, out of the dark house, and into the darker night.

As Edgar crept nearer the toolbox, his feet made squishing sounds in the soft, wet earth. He heard low, rumbling snores coming from the shed. Edgar knelt beside the toolbox and slowly lifted its lid.

Crreeeaaakk!

Edgar's stomach clenched. He listened closely, but Heimertz's snores continued uninterrupted. Edgar held his breath and quietly rummaged through the tools. His fingers found a familiar shape near the bottom and, clutching the wrench tightly, he fled.

In his haste to get away, Edgar didn't notice that Heimertz's snoring had ceased and that the caretaker's ramshackle shed was as still as the cricketless night. Nor did he see the glowing smile that floated behind the shed's single cracked window.

13. Preparing for Disaster

With dawn still hours away, the twins sneaked out of their backyard and into the neighborhood, snaking through the maze of sleeping houses. Edgar had stocked his satchel with new supplies, and Ellen carried a crusty shovel over her shoulder. Both clutched paint cans and brushes. Moving through deep shadows toward the center of town, the two slipped unseen by the few citizens still sweeping sidewalks and watering flower beds.

They turned a corner and came face-to-face with the Poshi family's freshly clipped hedges. Leafy replicas of Mr. Poshi, Mrs. Poshi, and little Timmy and Pepper

Poshi waved cheerfully to the twins. Even the berry bush was trimmed to look like the Poshis' cocker spaniel.

"No plant deserves that kind of humiliation," Edgar said. "I feel it is our duty to put those hedges out of their misery." He picked up the clippers, which still lay on the grass.

As her brother attacked the greenery, Ellen spied Roxy, Mrs. Jackson's basset hound with the French poodle hairdo, sleeping outside her newly decorated doghouse next door. Ellen untied the purple bow on Roxy's tail, being careful not to wake the dog, and returned to Edgar's side. He had nearly finished with the clippers.

"You know, Sister," he said, viciously swiping at Pepper's upraised hand, "there's one problem with this whole plan: Stephanie. She could ruin everything."

"We just need to keep her occupied with other things," Ellen said, casually dropping the ribbon on top of her brother's hedge trimmings.

"Hurry up, Edgar. We have lots of stops to make, and this night won't last forever."

They split up when they reached the river, and Ellen headed for the Hotel Motel. She stashed her equipment in the lobby and tiptoed down the inn's dark corridors, sliding handwritten notes beneath the tourists' doors.

Something moved at the far end of the hall, and Ellen stood up straight and still. A willowy woman in a white gown materialized out of the gloom, her slippered feet silent on the carpeting. Ellen wished Edgar were there; he had always wanted to see a ghost.

"Can't you see it?" the phantom asked.

As she floated toward Ellen, gesturing gracefully to unseen objects, Ellen realized with some disappointment that this ghostly form was solid flesh. Nora de Groot was sleepwalking.

And sleep talking.

"Can't you see it?" she asked, louder this time.

"Shhhh," Ellen hissed.

"Can't you *see it*?"

Ellen was afraid these cries would wake the hotel guests before she could finish her deliveries, so she searched for a soothing lullaby to lure Nora de Groot back to her bed. Most lullabies made her want to vomit, but thoughts of a tortured Berenice strengthened her resolve, and she recalled one that Edgar sang to Pet when they were younger. Ellen began to sing softly, all the while steering Nora de Groot back down the corridor:

Rock-a-bye baby, in the treetop,
Hope you don't tumble; it's quite a drop.
What are you doing, trying to fly?
You'll soar and you'll sail,
'Til you fall down and die.

Crooning the final note of her lullaby, Ellen shoved the sleepwalker back inside her room.

Meanwhile, across town Edgar slipped Heimertz's wrench back into his satchel and surveyed his handiwork at the Museum of Wax.

He looked over his shoulder at the motionless figures. "Might want to take off that jacket," he said to a nearby statue. "It's going to get a little warm in here."

He headed south and rejoined his sister in the park.

"Everything's set at the museum. Any trouble at the motel? Ellen? Hey, *pimpletoes!*"

Ellen was staring across the street.

"Look at that," she said.

Next to Town Hall a chain-link fence encircled an enormous wooden barricade.

"The bigger the fence, the better the secret," said Edgar, eyeing the KEEP OUT signs. "Let's see what Knightleigh has planned for his French Toast Festival."

The twins prowled along the base of the barricade. Scaling it was out of the question—not only was it too high, but Knightleigh's team had also greased the lower levels of fencing to discourage curious townspeople.

"Too bad those birds can't tell us what's inside," said Ellen, looking at some pigeons perched high atop the fence, clucking and fluffing their feathers.

"If only we had a catapult," said Edgar.

"We could fling you right in there," agreed Ellen.

They examined the fence gate, which was not so much a gate as a heavy steel door with three dead bolts and nine padlocks.

"I don't have enough keys in my satchel for all these locks," Edgar scowled.

"How are we going to get in?" asked Ellen. "Sunrise isn't far off, and we still have lots to do."

Edgar cracked his knuckles, and then remembered Ellen's shovel.

"We tunnel," he said.

They found a patch of uneven ground at the back of the site. Ellen had barely started digging when the sound of a dog barking startled the twins. It burst through the still night, moving closer.

"Does the mayor have guard dogs around this thing?" whispered Edgar.

Before Ellen could respond, a shaggy sheepdog bounded around the side of the fence and halted in front of the twins. It stopped barking and started growling.

"Dudley! Get back here. Where are you?" A woman rounded the corner after the dog. "Oh." The twins recognized Nancy Weedle, a writer for the *Nod's Limbs Gazette*. "What are you two kids doing out at this hour—with a shovel—digging by the mayor's top-secret area?"

"Sewer repair, ma'am. We're just wrapping things up," said Ellen, tugging on Edgar's pajamas as he quickly gathered up their gear. "Have a nice walk. Lovely mongrel you've got there." The twins left the confused woman and her growling dog at the fence.

"Wrapping things up?" snapped Edgar. "I want to see what's inside."

"Digging will take all night!" Ellen replied. "Besides, we have plans of our own, and they'll beat anything the mayor has stashed inside his little fortress. Come on— let's get back to work."

The twins left Town Hall and walked along the Running River. Seven covered bridges shimmered in the moonlight, and when they reached the western-most bridge, they could read the message painted on the seven rooftops facing them: COME BACK SOON FRIEND AND TAKE CARE.

"Ha!" said Ellen, arming herself with a paintbrush. "No one will want to come back here anytime soon."

The twins scrambled up the side of the first bridge and went to work. Several hours later, after they had climbed across all seven bridges and visited the last few necessary locales around Nod's Limbs, everything was finally in place. The first rays of sunlight broke the night sky, and although they were tired, Edgar and Ellen skipped home, shaking sand from their threadbare pajamas.

14. Earlier to Rise

By 8:30 that morning, the tourists had assembled in the lobby of the Hotel Motel.

"What kind of game is this Knightleigh guy running?" Blake Glide asked hotly, waving one of Ellen's notes in front of him. "Slipping this under the door in the middle of the night, telling us to be here *half an hour earlier* than we'd been told? On the set, no one dares to call me before 10 A.M.!"

"Did everyone else notice the awkward energy force of these rooms?" asked Nils de Groot. "We had to blow into our wind chimes for forty-five minutes to get the positive channels flowing."

"I didn't notice any energy force," said Alex Sai. "But that *does* explain the annoying tinkling sound that kept me awake." She glowered at the lobby's peeling wallpaper through her blue-tinted sunglasses.

"Where's my espresso?" she snapped. Alex Sai had very little patience before she had her morning coffee. Alex Sai had very little patience even *after* she had her morning coffee.

Only Mary Feemore seemed chipper and awake.

"I just love mornings, don't you?" she asked the journalist. Alex Sai gave her a nasty look.

The lobby doors swung open.

In stomped Ellen, wearing a black hat and a badge that read TOUR GUIDE. She held a tour book in one hand and a baton in the other. In fact, it looked more like a ratty mop than a baton; it was really Pet lashed to the top of an old rake. Edgar followed behind, carrying his satchel.

"Chop-chop, people!" Ellen shouted. The sleepy group responded slowly, so she blew the whistle that hung around her neck. This got everyone's attention.

"Listen up," Ellen started again, "I am your official tour guide for the day, and this is my assistant." She pointed to Edgar. "He will assure safe passage from site to site, because we, of course, do not want any unfortunate accidents to befall the lot of you."

"Greetings," Edgar said.

"Accidents?" asked Alex Sai. "This town doesn't seem so dangerous."

"Oh, you'd be surprised," answered Edgar.

"He doesn't look like much of a bodyguard, does he, dear?" whispered Nora de Groot to her husband.

"What's with the mop?" asked Blake Glide.

"So you can see me in a crowd," Ellen said. "We need to stay together."

"What's that yellow thing on top?" asked Mary Feemore.

"It's an eye, so I can always see *you* in a crowd," said Ellen.

Mary Feemore shivered.

"Repulsive," said Alex Sai.

"We have a lot of territory to cover, so we'd best be on our way before you waste any more of my time." Ellen blasted her whistle again. "Move it, move it."

The tour members fell in line and followed Ellen out the door.

"Where is our tour bus?" asked Nora de Groot.

"Oh, there will be no bus today," said Ellen.

"What? This is *most* inconvenient," said Nils de Groot. "These delicate shoes were handmade in Italy by a renowned cobbler and were not intended for walking."

"You'll see that Nod's Limbs is best experienced at ground level," said Ellen. "Otherwise, you would miss the hidden details, the little things that make this place tick...tick...*tick*."

"But I'm famous," protested Blake Glide. "I never walk anywhere."

"Honestly, I don't know which is worse—small-town tours or small-town tourists," said Alex Sai. "Let's get this over with."

"Forward march!" said Ellen.

"If we build a hotel here, a new pair of shoes is going on our expense account," said Nils de Groot.

Edgar and Ellen led the group down Copenhagen Lane, singing an encouraging song to themselves as they went:

> *Off we take our guests to see*
> *A tour of pure insanity;*
> *We'll shock these famous VIPs*
> *'Til they're about to crack—*
> *These unsuspecting visitors*
> *Have no idea we're saboteurs.*
> *They'll see a town of crazy curs*
> *And never dare come back!*

15. Too Late

Less than half an hour after Edgar and Ellen commandeered the tour, Stephanie Knightleigh strutted into the lobby of the Hotel Motel. She was surprised to find it empty. Had every single tourist slept late?

"Celebrities," she muttered. "Maybe the Elines know where everyone is."

The Elines were the elderly couple who ran the Hotel Motel. Stephanie found them sitting outside on the back porch.

"Where are all the tourists?" Stephanie demanded.

"Why, with the guides, of course," Mrs. Elines answered in a tiny voice. "Can I get you some tea?" she asked.

"What do you mean, 'They're with the guides'? I'm the guide. See my badge?" And, indeed, she wore a paper badge that read OFFICIAL HISTORICAL GUIDE.

"They were little gremlin twins, my dear, in striped pajamas," Mr. Elines explained.

"WHAT?" Stephanie yelled and the Elines jumped. "You mean, *those two* kidnapped my tour?" Her face turned a bright shade of strawberry. "That doll-murdering troublemaker is trying to ruin my life!"

"The girl had a mop with her, I remember," Mrs.

Elines said. "Are you sure you wouldn't like some nice chamomile to calm you down?"

"They're going to pay for this!" exclaimed Stephanie, shaking her fists to the heavens before clomping down Copenhagen Lane.

"Strange girl," said Mrs. Elines.

"Mmm, yes," replied her husband.

16. A Day at the Beach

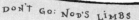

DON'T GO: NOD'S LIMBS

THE BEACH

These days, when gazing at the homely brown expanse of the Nod's Limbs Beach, it's hard to imagine that once upon a time it was the glittering stronghold of buccaneers. That's right—ferocious swashbucklers of the sea! In olden days the Running River really ran, and booty-laden pirate boats navigated its swift rapids, often pausing for a brief rest on the Nod's Limbs waterfront. The encampments were the domain of captains both nasty and brutish, and a terrible fate befell any stranger who dared

tread near. As pirates and their captives began disappearing, fewer and
fewer ships chose this particular
riverbank for their stopovers. No one
knows what happened to those pirates,
but a local legend attributes their
disappearance to something called the
"Limbsless Monster." If you put your
ear to the sand, sometimes you can
still hear their haunted cries.

The Nod's Limbs Beach was not so much a riverfront resort as a small plot of rough sand, begun when
a horse-drawn cart lost a wheel and accidentally
dumped a pile of the stuff there years before. The
then-mayor liked the idea of a beach in Nod's Limbs
and ordered more cartloads of sand, figuring that the
townspeople might enjoy building sand castles, sunbathing, and surfing. Surfing was a problem, because
the Running River did not have waves, or much
water at all for that matter, but sand castle building
and sunbathing were quite popular in the summer.

Today no one reclined on the beach, and all the
sand castles had been stomped out.

As the visitors approached, Nora de Groot turned
to her husband and said, "Can't you see it, darling?

What this shoreline needs is a hexagonal beach house sculpted from sand, held aloft by six thermoplastic buttresses. In red, I think."

"Wouldn't your sand house wash away when it rains?" asked Mary Feemore.

"That's the whole point," said Nora de Groot. "The supports would remain, like the mountains. It's a comment about the impermanence of society."

"Never mind her, my lovely," her husband said. "Your genius is not meant to be understood by everyone." The pair exchanged a warm glance.

Ellen stopped the group on the sidewalk, just short of the beach, and blew her whistle.

"Welcome to Nod's Limbs Beach," she said. "Way back in the nineteenth century, marauding pirates used this area as a rest stop between pillaging trips. You might want to watch your step, people."

She aimed Pet, whose single eye was now covered with a leather eye patch, at a jagged wooden sign that read BEWARE LESSIE—ENTER AT YOUR OWN RISK. A tattered sun hat rested at the base of the sign.

"Ah, a fresh victim," said Ellen. "Poor soul."

"Is this some kind of joke?" asked Alex Sai.

"Someone fell in here this morning?" asked Blake Glide.

"Someone was *dragged* in here this morning," said Ellen. "Townsfolk tell of a mysterious creature who dwells in the quicksand. The Limbsless Monster is said to be a snakelike beast that prowls our riverfront for human meals."

"I don't want to hear about urban legends...suburban legends...whatever legends you bumpkins believe," said Alex Sai. "I need facts."

"We should call an ambulance," cried Mary Feemore.

Ellen sighed. "Goodness, no; there's no sense in an ambulance now. That luckless dear is long, *long* gone."

A dumbstruck silence fell over the group.

"Wait a minute—where is your assistant?" asked Mary Feemore, looking around for Edgar.

"The monster got him!" gasped Blake Glide.

"Perhaps," said Ellen. "I sent him ahead to scout the river for signs of old Lessie. Being eaten by a murderous beast might spoil your tour."

The tourists were silent again. They seemed unsure how to respond to this information.

"Don't worry, Ms. Sai," Blake Glide said finally. "I fought a killer Gila monster in my film *Death Valley High*. I'm sure I can handle something limbless." He gave her a dramatic wink.

"Probably not," warned Ellen. "There are no known survivors of Lessie's attacks. Its deadliness is legendary. The pirates who long ago sailed these waters made their captives walk the plank, not into the river, but into the creature's quicksand lair, a much more gruesome death. Sometimes, if you listen closely, you can still hear the victims' cries of anguish...."

The group quieted, but all they heard was the sound of the river trickling past.

Suddenly, a low wail rose from the shore.

"Help meeee...save meeee...I don't want to diiiie...," the voice trailed off into a muffled moan.

"What was that?" asked Blake Glide. He looked quickly from Ellen to the waterfront and back.

"Ghosts—voices of the dead—they speak to me! Do you hear them as well?" asked Nora de Groot.

"I should hope we can all hear them. That racket's giving me a headache," said Alex Sai.

"They are the lost souls, victims of Lessie," said Ellen, "forever trying to lure others into the jaws of the beast."

"Surely not!" said Mary Feemore.

"I'm not falling for it," said Blake Glide, who nevertheless took a step back.

Alex Sai turned to Ellen. "If this place is so dangerous," she said, "why hasn't anyone caught this monster and cleared away the quicksand?"

"Oh, the mayor thinks it's handy for tax evaders," replied Ellen.

"The mayor——?" asked Mary Feemore.

"And parents find it helpful for threatening disobedient children," Ellen continued.

The wailing had started again.

"Mother, where have you gone? Where——?"

"Horrid!" exclaimed Nora de Groot in a shaky voice. "I will build no beach house here. The karmic balance is *disturbed*."

Mary Feemore scribbled furiously on her notepad. Alex Sai, however, stepped gingerly onto the sand.

"Where *is* that voice coming from?" she asked.

"Aiiiiieeeeeeeee!"

The piercing scream ripped through the air and echoed off the boulders lining the shore. Alex Sai covered her ears and moved back a few feet.

"I insist that we depart at once," said Nils de Groot, stepping away.

"No sense dawdling," said Blake Glide, stumbling over the architect as he scuttled backward.

"Of course. We have much more to see," said Ellen. "Ahoy maties!" She marched off down Copenhagen

Lane. Alex Sai gave one last glance at the sand and followed the retreating tour.

17. Not Quick Enough

As Ellen led the tourists away, Edgar slipped from behind the boulders. Holding a tin can, he followed the length of the attached hose to the center of the beach, unearthed it, and coiled it over his shoulder. At the other end of the hose, a second tin can just poked up through the sand.

Edgar returned the intercom to his satchel, turned the LESSIE sign around, and ducked behind a boulder to wait.

Soon, an out-of-breath Stephanie sprinted up to the beach, finding nothing but the abandoned beach hat and a sign that read DETOUR: VIP PHOTO SHOOT THIS WAY.

"Why wasn't I informed of a photo shoot?" she demanded. "This is my tour! I should be in the pictures!" She stormed off in the direction the hand-drawn arrow pointed.

"Ha!" said Edgar. "That was easier than catching Pet." He hurried after Ellen and the tour group.

Stephanie, meanwhile, followed Nassau Way, looking for the tourists. But after reaching the end of the road, she had seen no sign of them. Nassau led her right to Town Hall, where much activity was still taking place behind the enormous construction barricade. A crowd of curious citizens had gathered around it, chattering.

"I bet it's an automated scoreboard for the Nod's Limbs O-limb-pics—one of those fancy Jumbotrons! Old Man Barger always falls asleep up in the stands and forgets to change the scores by hand."

"No, it's probably a jungle gym for the grammar school. My little Adam will be thrilled. There's such overcrowding, the kids have to play in shifts!"

Just then Mayor Knightleigh stepped out from the top-secret area, talking to a contractor. He caught sight of his daughter.

"Stephanie!" he exclaimed. "What are you doing here?" He pulled her aside and whispered, *"Where are our important guests?"*

"Oh…well…ah…the tourists are—," Stephanie stammered.

"Young lady, need I remind you how crucial this day is? Our application for recognition in the National Registry of Historic Treasures depends on those VIPs—Alex Sai in particular. That listing in the NRHT will bring thousands of tourists here."

"I know, Daddy. Everything is under control. I just...ah...wanted to report to you that everything is going well. No need to worry. But I'll get back to our guests right now," Stephanie said.

"You do that, my girl. Remember, you are a Knightleigh, and that name will be world-renowned once we build the Knightlorian! When your mother returns from her business trip next week, she will be pleased to hear that you're contributing to the family name. I don't want to see you again until the parade and the French Toast Festival!"

The mayor turned back to his contractor, and, fuming, Stephanie retraced her steps up Nassau Way.

18. Alien Invasion

As Edgar and Ellen led the tour down Copenhagen Lane, residents stood outside their homes smiling and waving. Blake Glide smiled and waved back.

"These good people have great taste!" he said. "It will be an honor to perform for them. We'll have shows every night in our theater and two on Sunday!" he said.

Alex Sai did not share his good cheer.

"I can't *believe* I let my boss send me here. *'Cities are so over, Alex. Small-town values are so vital, Alex....'*"

A small girl ran out of her house to greet the tour. She stopped short, however, when she saw who was guiding it.

"What are *you two* doing? I thought Stephanie was leading the tour," Annie Krump said.

"No autographs now," said Edgar. "Beat it." Ellen brandished her Pet-pole in Annie's face. The girl squeaked *"Eewww!"* and sprinted back inside.

Near the end of the block, the tourists halted in front of a sign that read THE POSHI FAMILY WELCOMES YOU. Mr. Poshi stood at the edge of his lawn, making a lot of noise. He wore a green vinyl protective suit and mask and held a large pesticide sprayer. Behind him his carefully trimmed hedge family now sported rake-thin bodies and enormous round heads.

"Who would do such a thing?" he cried, flapping his arms about. But the mask muffled his voice, and his words came out as a garbled *"Woodoosing, woodoosing!"*

"To the right," Ellen said, stopping the group and gesturing with her Pet-pole, "you will see the home of our resident alien family."

"Ah, aliens," said Nils de Groot. "Is this quaint village home to many nationalities? Bravo!"

"No. These aliens are from the planet Narshamp," Ellen explained, while Mr. Poshi continued yelling incoherently in the background. "That's what they say, anyway. For years the Poshi family has claimed that their people beamed them here to prepare earthlings for the Narshampian invasion. They go door-to-door, preaching the Narshampian way and handing out pamphlets with lots of diagrams and charts. Here is one now, standing next to a classic example of Narshampian shrubbery art. I believe he is trying to contact others on his planet as we speak. It may sound like gobbledygook to you, but in Narshampian, I think it means—," Ellen hesitated for a moment, "How are things going up there?"

Nora de Groot raised a single eyebrow and glanced at Ellen. "Little dear, you haven't fallen for this poor man's delusions too, have you?"

"I agree. He just looks like someone wearing a vinyl suit," Mary Feemore said. "Couldn't he come up with a better alien costume?"

"Perhaps you're right," said Ellen with a shrug. "He's just *so* convincing when he describes the Narshampian takeover of human bodies to use as vehicles here on Earth. They say the suits help the alien parasites control their human hosts."

"I fought alien parasites in *Misplaced in Space*," Blake Glide said. "Took 'em all out. If this guy bothers you, Ms. Sai, just say the word. I'll take him out, too."

Alex Sai rolled her eyes and turned to Ellen.

"Aren't the neighbors concerned that his questionable behavior could be dangerous?" she asked.

"Oh no," said Ellen. "Lots of his neighbors have started dressing in similar suits and passing out brochures."

"What?" cried Mary Feemore. "He is actually winning converts to his disturbed little cult?"

"I'm told the Narshampian lifestyle can really grow on you," Ellen said. "For the most part, they are a peaceful lot, except when people don't believe their story. Then they get a little hot tempered. Hmm. We might want to move along—it looks like it's time for him to spread the gospel."

Mr. Poshi looked wildly about and started coming toward the tourists, waving his shears and screaming, *"Who did this? Who did this to my family?"* With his mask on, however, it sounded more like *"Ooog ooog hoggie!"*

"Good heavens, Nils!" cried Nora de Groot. "Don't let him get his hands on me!"

As the visitors backed away from the raving pruner, another angry individual steamrolled through the neighbors gathered around the Poshi yard.

"Imposter!" Stephanie screeched, pointing at Ellen.

"Vandal!" hollered Ellen, pointing right back.

"WHAT?" shouted Mr. Poshi, which sounded like, "HRAAAPP!"

Edgar casually waved at the base of the hedges, where a purple silk ribbon lay among the strewn clippings. "I think the culprit left something behind."

Mr. Poshi stooped to pluck the ribbon from the ground and looked from it to similar ribbons in Stephanie's hair and back again. He tried to speak, but in his anger, he could only muster an "AAARRRCK!" which, coming through the mask, sounded like, "AAARRRCK!"

"It was you!" His neighbor, Mrs. Jackson, spoke up. "Your father will hear about this, young lady."

The crowd turned to look at Stephanie as she backed away from Mr. Poshi's accusing finger.

"I didn't do anything. I don't even know what you're talking about," she cried as the neighbors shook their heads.

"*Tsk tsk,* Stephanie. *Shame* on you," scolded Mrs. Jackson.

"It wasn't me! It was those twins!" Stephanie pleaded, looking around for Edgar and Ellen. But the twins had already whisked away the tourists, who had seemed eager to escape the close encounter.

Mr. Poshi and his neighbors encircled Stephanie, preventing her from following the tour group. With such compelling evidence in hand, they were unwilling to let the perpetrator flee.

19. Pestilence

DON'T GO: NOD'S LIMBS

DOWNTOWN

If you're looking for the next shopportunity or have a hankering for a local treat, head downtown. But buyer beware! The descendants of the pirates that sailed the Running River have run Nod's Limbs' commerce for generations, and their eating and retail establishments will welcome your wallet with open arms and nimble fingers. So when

```
that "brussels sprout soup in a bread
bowl" seems terribly expensive and you
say to your lunch companion, "That's
highway robbery!" don't worry—it is!
```

Edgar and Ellen hurried their group around the corner onto Brisbane Street and up to Mr. Barbarino's restaurant, where the owner waited outside.

"Welcome, welcome," he said. "Come and try Barbarino's 'Special of the Day.'" He wore a red-checkered apron and held a tray laden with sandwiches. Everyone eagerly gathered around him (the change in schedule had allowed no time for breakfast).

"Pardon me, Mr. Barbarino, but I think the group could use some coffee," said Ellen. "This boy will help you serve the food." She indicated Edgar. "And while you're at it, another round of sandwiches would be in order for my hungry friends."

"Absolutely! Anything to accommodate our important guests," the restaurant owner said.

"I'll go get more from your kitchen," said Edgar, and he disappeared into the building.

Mr. Barbarino pulled Ellen aside for a private word.

"Er...where's the mayor's daughter? I thought she was supposed to lead this tour."

"Oh, poor Stephanie was recently set upon by wild

dogs, and she is home recuperating. It's fortunate we were able to fill in on such short notice," Ellen said.

"Wild dogs! Really?" Mr. Barbarino said. "How unexpected."

Turning back to his guests, he announced, "Make sure you save some room for the winners at the French Toast Festival this afternoon—my special recipe is in the cook-off!"

Edgar reappeared with the tray and offered it to each of the tourists, who greedily gobbled up the sandwiches. Even Alex Sai was famished enough to tuck into a second one, bread and all. Edgar and Ellen refrained from dining; from atop its perch, Pet looked steadily at the food.

"Ah, subtle but engaging flavors," Nora de Groot enthused. "I must get the recipe and pass it along to our nutritionist."

"A deep hint of exotic spices with a Mediterranean flair," agreed Nils de Groot, dabbing at his lips with a napkin. "It's a modern interpretation of a classic."

Nora de Groot nodded her head. "Dear, you're clearly enjoying these treats—have you given up your all-plum diet?"

"Never. But you know how essential it is to try the local cuisine. It's part of the folk traditions that inform the constructed landscape," her husband replied. "What do you think inspired my pickle-shaped drive-through photo developer in Cleveland? The Ohio gherkin!"

Ellen said, "Mr. Barbarino is known for using only the freshest ingredients."

"You are so kind. It is my pleasure to feed very important persons such as yourselves," the restaurant owner said. "I'll go get the coffee." He went inside.

"I wonder what ingredient in these sandwiches makes them crunch so delightfully," Mary Feemore said.

She looked down to examine hers and watched a small cockroach scuttle out of it onto her hand. A stream of black ants followed the bug, marching onto her wrist and up her arm.

"*Aah!*"

"What's wrong?" Alex Sai said, turning to see.

"AAAAH!" Mary Feemore screamed again, violently shaking her hand and catapulting the roach and ants onto her fellow journalist.

"What are you doing?" Alex Sai cried, swatting the insects from her shirt. Only then did she observe what was escaping from her own sandwich.

"*AAAAH!*" shrieked Alex Sai.

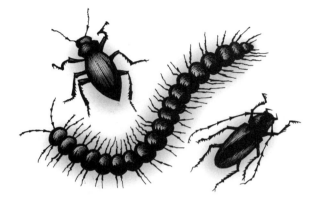

The rest of the guests joined in the squealing as bugs crawled out of their food, and they spat out what they had praised just seconds earlier. Blake Glide turned a sickly shade, and Nora de Groot clawed at her tongue.

When Mr. Barbarino reappeared with the coffee-pot, he was alarmed to see his guests racing off.

"Wait! *Wait!* You forgot your coffee!" he yelled after them.

"We don't want any of your coffee, you sicko!" Alex Sai shouted back.

They fled down the street and into a park near the center of town, a pleasant place where shoppers and workers stopped to rest and admire the river view. Benches surrounded a beautiful garden and a water fountain, which Mary Feemore, gagging and holding her stomach, was the first to spot. The tourists frantically lined up to rinse the foul lunch from their mouths.

The twins lagged behind.

"Fantastic, Brother. Tourists won't come to Nod's Limbs for *that* local delicacy," said Ellen.

"Compliments of Berenice's lunch pail, Sister," Edgar replied. "Insect finger sandwiches—*La Spécialité du Gadget Graveyard.*"

> *A shame they missed our best cuisine:*
> *Cockroach à la lima beans!*
> *Still, a brilliant range of greens*
> *Is spread across their faces.*
> *They surely won't be coming back*
> *After such a crawly snack.*
> *We'll keep our junkyard; they'll unpack*
> *Their lives in other places.*

20. What's in a Name?

As Alex Sai leaned against the water fountain, heaving and wiping her mouth, she noticed a dozen or so pigeons swoop in and land on an imposing statue at the other side of the park.

"Who's that?" she asked hoarsely. Atop a wide concrete pedestal was a sculpture that looked cast from solid gold. A regal man in a waistcoat sat erect upon an ornate chair. The tourists gaped at his golden brilliance, but soon focused on another, more puzzling feature. The statue had no limbs.

"That's Nod," Ellen answered, "the founder of our town."

"What happened to his arms and legs?" Mary Feemore asked.

Ellen hesitated. The statue wasn't on the tour, and she hadn't planned any remarks about it, and truthfully, no one knew the story of what happened to Nod's limbs. So she invented her own.

"Local legend tells that when Nod founded the settlement, he called it 'Nod's Bod.' But his arms and legs got tired of always doing what Nod wanted to do. Nod was a pushy sort of fellow, and one day they just up and walked away. Well, the arms had to crawl away. The legs strolled about town entertaining the people by doing little jigs, while the arms waved and shook everybody's hands. They ended up being more popular than Nod himself, so the citizens changed the village's name to Nod's Limbs."

"So why isn't there a statue of Nod's arms and legs?" asked Mary Feemore.

"Because one day they simply disappeared. And only a limbless Nod was left to pose for the sculptor."

"That doesn't make sense," said Alex Sai.

"Oh, don't try to make sense of it," said Ellen. "More than a few citizens have gone mad that way."

Blake Glide whispered to Alex Sai, "Maybe that's what happened to the Narshampian."

At the base of the statue, a plaque read NOD: FOUNDER OF NOD'S LIMBS, 1742–?

"Why is there no date for his death?" Alex Sai asked.

"*He* disappeared too," Ellen said. "If he died, no one ever found a body. People have seen his arms and legs, though. They roam the Black Tree Forest, forever searching for the body of Nod so they can reunite as one."

"If they find him, he'd be over two hundred years old," Alex Sai said with a snort. "What, was he an alien, too?"

The tourists chuckled nervously. Ellen just grinned and then loudly blew her whistle, making Alex Sai wince. "Enough dillydallying, people. We've got a museum to see."

As they walked back toward the street, Ellen saw a purple streak fly past the park's front gate.

21. Hot on the Trail

After escaping Mr. Poshi and his angry neighbors, Stephanie ran to Mr. Barbarino's. When the distressed restaurant owner told her the VIPs had moved on, she headed straight to the Museum of Wax, the next stop on the tour. But there she found no one. The museum was closed to the public so the special guests could have a private viewing.

"They can't have come and gone already," she grumbled and sat down to wait outside the museum's entrance.

But Stephanie was not alone.

Edgar had hurried ahead of the tour to check on the museum, and looking out a second-floor window, he saw her climb the hill to the building's entrance.

"*Hmm*—a bit ahead of schedule," he murmured. He took a rope from his satchel and tossed one end high into the air so that it looped around a rafter. Edgar opened the window and stuck his head out.

"Hey, Stephanie! Heard you lost something this morning!" He ducked back into the building.

"Ooo! Weasel!" Stephanie growled and raced in after Edgar, abandoning her post at the door just as Ellen and the tourists started walking up the hill.

22. Museum du Jour

DON'T GO: NOD'S LIMBS

MUSEUM OF WAX

A major attraction in the downtown area is the Nod's Limbs Museum of Wax, a monument to the art of inflicting pain. The original building housed a gallery, courthouse, and jail, where punishments were meted out for misdeeds big and small. The town stopped the ancient practice of scaring confessions out of offenders by dipping them in hot wax when some of the "temporary exhibits" accidentally became part of the "permanent collection."

"I'm eager to see this museum," said Mary Feemore. "I've heard it displays some of the region's most daring accomplishments in wax art."

"I don't care if it displays some of the region's most daring accomplishments in tax accounting—I just want to go on a *normal* tour of a *normal* museum," Alex Sai replied.

The Nod's Limbs Museum of Wax was the community's prized institution. Unlike most wax museums, which feature replicas of celebrities, historical figures, and notorious criminals, Nod's Limbs' wax museum had replicas of the town of Nod's Limbs. For just ten dollars an entry—half off for children!—visitors could view wax imitations of what they had just seen outside. For example, one room was dedicated to the Nod's Limbs Grammar School. The fourth-grade teacher, Miss Croquet, often led field trips to the museum to see the wax version of herself standing at the head of the classroom, while twenty wax students sat at their wax desks. The museum made most of its money from citizens who came to admire wax models of themselves.

"Right this way," Ellen ordered after a sharp toot on her whistle. "We haven't got all day."

She swung open the doors, and a swell of hot air greeted the tour. Something was dreadfully wrong.

The first exhibit was the Hall of Mayors, which usually featured two rows of well-dressed men sporting identical beady eyes—wax models of every Knightleigh to govern Nod's Limbs, from Thaddeus to the current mayor. But standing before the tourists were not replicas of distinguished gentlemen from bygone eras, but rather bubbly, disfigured human forms. Faces had melted into simmering messes, leaving only glass eyeballs atop streaming mounds of wax. Fingers had softened into dripping cones hanging from skeletal wrists.

Edgar, with the help of Heimertz's wrench, had turned up the furnace full blast. The life-size statues looked like candles after a long dinner party. Wax ran over the mayors' cloth suits and onto the ground, pooling beside top hats and fedoras.

"Ah, the contemporary art museum," sighed Nils de Groot. "At last, a place where I can connect."

"Yes," said Nora de Groot, "I haven't seen modern art like this since…since…*my goodness,* I've never seen modern art like this. It's rather provocative—almost *disturbing.*"

"Why, whatever do you mean?" Ellen asked. "This is Thaddeus Knightleigh, Nod's Limbs' first and longest-reigning mayor." She held up her guidebook for everyone to see. Next to the description of the first mayor was a picture of the Creature from the Black Lagoon emerging from the swamp, traced from *The Gruesome Guide to Gory Movies.* Everyone huddled in to get a closer look.

"I had no idea when I agreed to consider this project that Nod's Limbs had such a, *ah,* unique population," Nils de Groot said. "It does pose some design challenges."

"Indeed," Ellen said, "the citizens of Nod's Limbs have a long history of genetic disorders."

They next entered the grammar-school classroom, where Miss Croquet's eyeballs had sunk into her nose. Her lips drooped in a wide frown which hung to her shoulders. Her students looked like reflections frozen in a fun-house mirror.

"This is one of Nod's Limbs' most cherished teachers. She is a great influence in children's lives."

"What happened to her?" Mary Feemore asked.

"No one knows for sure," Ellen replied, "but there are rumors."

"Oh great, more fairy tales," said Alex Sai.

"It's said that when Miss Croquet was young, she was a brilliant scientist—an expert in tropical diseases— and she would have won the Nobel Prize if one of her experiments hadn't gone terribly, horribly wrong."

"How wrong?" asked Alex Sai.

"She created a new disease," Ellen said.

"You mean she discovered one?" asked Mary Feemore.

"No, she *created* a new disease," Ellen repeated. "And she gave it to herself. It's a contagious skin disorder. The experience left her mentally unstable, and now she's trying to find a formula to restore her health. As you can see, the students assist in her work."

"Are you saying she experiments on…on…her *students*?" Mary Feemore asked.

"Well, let's just say those kids didn't walk in looking like that," said Ellen. "It's a privilege, really. Miss Croquet was, after all, a Nobel honorable mention."

23. Wax On

Meanwhile, Stephanie stood in the second-floor gallery that represented a day at the public pool. Normally, wax citizens sunbathed and frolicked in the wax water, but now drifting chunks of inner tube and snorkel gear floated past the melted diving board. Stephanie had no reason to look up when so much around her was in ruin. If she had, she would have seen Edgar perched on a rafter.

With a shrill "TO THE DEPTHS!" Edgar seized his rope and plummeted toward the startled girl.

She had no time to run, no chance to duck. Edgar knocked Stephanie headfirst into the murky pool.

The noise brought the tourists running up the stairs. Edgar left his rope dangling and stood waiting for them.

"Enjoying the tour?" he asked innocently.

A gurgling commotion came from the pool as Stephanie emerged and tried to wade to a ladder. She was covered head to foot in blue, lumpy wax.

"What in heaven's name is that?" yelled Blake Glide. He stepped back, tripping over Alex Sai.

"Relax," said Ellen. "This is just...Prunella Crudley, one of Miss Croquet's former students. She's a docent here and gives in-depth tours of the collection. Looks like she wants to show you around. Isn't that right, Prunella?"

Struggling through the muck, Stephanie tried to talk, but the wax had sealed her lips shut.

"What's wrong, Prunella? Got wax in your ears?" snickered Edgar.

"This place...this *place*—what is *wrong* with this *place*?" cried Nora de Groot.

Blake Glide stood pressed against the wall. "She better not come near me! My skin is insured, but filming for *Lethally Handsome* starts next week!"

"Let's move along now," Ellen said. "We're still not sure how contagious she is. Just a precaution; nothing to worry about." Not one of them noticed Edgar slipping away, taking a shortcut to the next landmark.

The tourists, clinging to one another, needed no encouragement to file quickly down the stairs and out of the building.

24. Hirschfeld Muses

Stephanie made it up the ladder and out of the pool. Abandoned in the gallery, she trudged downstairs to the schoolroom in search of a towel, leaving a trail of dripping sludge behind her. When Stephanie caught her reflection in a window, she groaned. She didn't look much better off than the wax teacher.

"Alas, what has happened?"

Stephanie wheeled around to see Mr. Hirschfeld, the museum's longtime custodian, standing in the doorway.

"Miss Knightleigh...is that you? What have you done?" he asked pitifully, with a hand to his forehead. "Look at this place! I have spent decades tending this collection of masterpieces, and now—*how grievous*—in a day it's beyond repair. Not from neglect…decay… carelessness…

"But from the spite of a child."

He knelt in front of the melting Miss Croquet. "Here stood the esteemed educator whom I dusted I know not how often. Where is your wise counsel now? Your quiet genius?"

He rose and turned on Stephanie. "A museum's mandate is to serve the public! Do you presume ownership of this place, merely because you're a *Knightleigh*? Is it a *lark* for you to spoil someone else's sweat and toil? I saw what you did to Poshi's hedge!"

Stephanie picked enough wax from her lips to respond. "I didn't do it!" she protested. "It was those horrible twins in the dirty pajamas! They kidnapped my tour!"

"Young lady, you should be ashamed, laying the blame on others. No one else is here! Someone needs to teach you some manners. You will help me clean this up!"

Mr. Hirschfeld handed Stephanie a bucket and scraper. "Now get to it!"

If her wax-caked knees had been easier to bend, she might have bolted from the room, but she was far too crusty to make a clean getaway.

25. Who Wants a Crabby Apple?

DON'T GO: NOD'S LIMBS

CRABBY APPLE TREE

The most attractive sight along the
stretch of Cairo Avenue known to locals
as "the Dullest Part of Town" is the
famed Crabby Apple Tree. Some years
back the current mayor's grandfather,
who was just as irritating as his
grandson, saved the tree from the chipper. Long before and long since, its
twisted branches and thick cover of
leaves have provided shade and shelter
to generations of picnickers and
escaped criminals.

Ellen led the group to busy Cairo Avenue. She
stopped inches from the speedy flow of traffic and
gestured at a gnarled tree that looked like it grew
right out of the road. On closer inspection, however,
the visitors could see that the two-lane avenue split at
the tree, one lane veering tightly to its left and the
other veering closely to its right.

The Crabby Apple Tree was the most famous tree in
all of Nod's Limbs: legend said that Nod himself had

once tied his horse to it. Years ago, when the original plans for Cairo Avenue called for the removal of the tree, community support for the landmark was so great that the mayor decreed the road should go around the tree. And so they built it, literally, around the tree.

Cars and trucks whipped past, and the tourists drew back from the curb. Drivers in Nod's Limbs rarely exceeded the speed limit; however, when permitted by law to accelerate all the way to thirty-five miles per hour (which they could on Cairo Avenue), they took full advantage of the opportunity.

"Listen up, people," said Ellen over the noisy traffic. "Step where I step, and jump where I jump, and you should make it to the tree in one piece."

"Are you crazy? I'm not chasing you into traffic!" said Alex Sai.

"Well, you're welcome to stay here...out in the open...by yourselves. I'm sure Prunella will be along any minute to keep you company."

The shaken group looked back in the direction of the museum. No one was approaching—yet.

"You really must come along. Otherwise you'll miss something *very* special. Now, please be careful," Ellen warned. "The Nod's Limbs maintenance crew has to remove corpses of the unfortunates who don't cross quickly enough. I'd hate to have to summon them for any of you."

With that she darted through the traffic.

"Haven't these loons heard of a traffic light?" yelled Alex Sai.

"What dreadful urban planning!" screeched the de Groots, cowering together.

"CORPSES?" screamed Blake Glide.

The group followed Ellen as best they could, cautiously weaving through the cars. Many of the drivers honked and waved when they recognized the celebrities dodging their vehicles.

"Loved you in *Fatal Bludgeon 4*!" the driver of an oncoming minivan shouted at Blake Glide. Blake valiantly flashed a thumbs-up while barely saving himself from certain death.

"That was distinctly undignified," said Nils de Groot once they finally reached the safety of the tree.

"At least it will keep us hidden from that diseased docent. I do feel sorry for her," said Nora de Groot, placing her cheek against the Crabby Apple Tree. "Let us be thankful for our health and for nature's protection."

"Tell me again why we're stopping here," Alex Sai said, "to see a tree in the middle of the road?"

The frazzled group seemed unimpressed. It was just an average crab apple tree.

"As you can see, this tree is famous," Ellen said, pointing with her Pet-pole to an engraved plaque at its base:

OUR BELOVED CRABBY APPLE TREE

Here Nod tied his horse after his first crossing of the Running River and envisioned an empire made of wax.

"You want famous trees? They put a plaque on the trees I swung from in *My Man Tarzan*. I did all my own stunts in that film," said Blake Glide. "Would you like to go up, Ms. Sai? Your shoes look like they weren't made for climbing, so I could carry you."

"No thanks, ham hock," Alex Sai said, and she looked over her blue-tinted sunglasses at Ellen. "I didn't travel all the way to Nod's Limbs to see a tree. I can't believe I am supposed to write about this asylum that calls itself a town—this story's not fit to print. Can we move on, please, so I can get this day over with?"

As Alex Sai spoke, Mary Feemore gazed up into the tree's leaves and saw something move among the branches.

"Miss…um, Tour Guide—there's someone in the tree."

"I'm sure it's just a squirrel," said Ellen.

"But I could swear it was striped," Mary Feemore said.

"I know what you're thinking," said Ellen. "However, I can assure you that what you saw definitely *isn't* an escaped convict from the maximum security prison outside town."

"Escaped convict?" asked Blake Glide. "Come again?"

"The rumors are true," Ellen admitted with a sigh. "The night-duty jailer sometimes falls asleep on the job. He's the mayor's cousin so he'll never get fired. Runaway criminals often find their way to this tree because it is such a convenient source of food and shelter."

"Egad!" cried Nils de Groot.

"Not to worry," said Ellen. "When one escapes, our mayor personally sounds the siren outside Town Hall. But escapes hardly ever happen. It's been weeks since the last one."

"Atrocious," said Nora de Groot. "Where is the enraged outcry of the citizenry? Are they not furious about this poorly guarded jail in their midst?"

"Oh no, they rather like escapees," said Ellen. "They're so entertaining. Most of our warmhearted locals look forward to an occasional visit from a shady felon with an ax."

At the very top of the Crabby Apple Tree, Edgar clung to the thin trunk, holding a long vacuum attachment hose scavenged from the Gadget Graveyard. He stretched his arm over the tips of the topmost branches and began to spin the hose. As it whirled, it began to hum and then to whine. The faster it spun, the more it sounded like a howl. Finally, at top velocity, the whizzing hose reached a piercing scream.

"The siren!" shrieked Blake Glide.

"People, people, please. No need to panic," assured Ellen. "Everything is under control."

"Where's our bodyguard?" demanded Nils de Groot.

"Perhaps we should move along," said Mary Feemore. She scribbled furiously in her notebook while casting anxious glances at the tree.

The siren stopped abruptly.

"See? There is absolutely nothing to worry about,"

said Ellen. "If a murderous convict were up there, he would have attacked us by now."

Suddenly, a torrent of crab apples rained down on the tourists. They threw their arms up to shield themselves.

"Run!" cried Nora de Groot, and they all bolted through the traffic, dodging the honks and screeching tires on Cairo Avenue as best they could.

"I don't want my investment overrun with escaped criminals!" Blake Glide cried as he ran.

"Final stop—the Nod's Limbs clock tower!" Ellen called out as the group reached the sidewalk. She blew on her whistle. "I promise; there won't be any prisoners there. Prisoners never hide out at the clock tower."

26. Blood Baths

DON'T GO: NOD'S LIMBS

CLOCK TOWER

It's best to experience the Nod's Limbs
clock tower on a cloudy day or at night,
when no sunshine can dispel the lingering horror of the executions that took
place there in olden times. But even on
a bright summer morning, it's still
worth a trip to the town's first multi-
story structure to run your fingers
over the many bloodstains where the
guillotine once stood.

Ellen hustled the tourists back across the river
toward the final stop of the day. All around them, citizens ran about in delirious anticipation, hanging flags
and streamers from lampposts and waving to the VIPs.
But the celebrities rubbed their bruises and saw only
criminal-harboring hooligans.

Nora de Groot fumed. "Miss Tour Guide, I have
had enough of this town. I have encountered nothing
but discord and disharmony since this tour began.
Please take us back to our lodgings."

"Yes, I've been threatened by space parasites, exposed to a contagious skin disease, and attacked with fruit," said Nils de Groot. "If you don't lead us back, we will find our own way."

"I agree," said Mary Feemore. "Those crab apples stained my blouse. I want to get out of here *right now*."

Ellen faced her guests. "Whoever threw those crab apples might come after us," she warned. "Don't be foolish. Stick with me. I'll lead you safely to the final stop on our tour." She marched off toward the clock tower.

Five tourists eyed one another, as if testing to see who was bold enough to set out for the Hotel Motel alone.

Five tourists broke into a trot to catch up with their guide.

Ellen heard them hustle up behind her and swung her Pet-pole in a wide arc above her head, causing Pet's single pupil to bounce back and forth like a pinball.

"Stop waving that thing around—you're attracting attention from the natives," whispered Nils de Groot.

Ellen pretended not to hear him.

"Here you see the famous Nod's Limbs clock

tower, where weekly executions took place," Ellen said as they reached the building.

"Executions?" Mary Feemore exclaimed.

"Oh yes," said Ellen. "Nod's Limbs is known for its history of intolerance toward intruders. Many were sentenced to have their heads chopped off."

Blake Glide instinctively clutched his own throat.

"Intruders like those escaped convicts?" asked Mary Feemore.

"No, folks around here like the convicts because they add to the town's unique charm," said Ellen. "But visitors who don't think nice thoughts about our quaint little Nod's Limbs—" Ellen paused, shrugged, and then shook her head.

"Let's head up the narrow, poorly lit staircase on my right to take advantage of the marvelous view," Ellen said, directing the visitors through the entrance. They reluctantly began to climb the steps single file just as Edgar arrived to stand lookout in front of the building. Ellen continued, "As you exit onto the roof, you can still see the bloodstains on the walls and floor right where the guillotine used to stand, until they moved it to the basement."

A splotchy red mess lay at the tourists' feet. It glistened slightly, as if it were still wet.

"That's a lot of blood," Blake Glide said. "That's more blood than I bled in *Fatal Bludgeon 7*, before I came back to life with newfound strength."

"Why haven't they cleaned it up?" asked Mary Feemore.

"Well, bloodstains are an art form in these parts, third only to the wax sculpting and shrubbery design you've been privileged to see. All the most fashionable home owners in Nod's Limbs try to achieve the same effect on their driveways."

"Finally, some local traditions I can write about," said Alex Sai. "When did they stop executing intruders?"

"Who said they stopped?"

27. Greetings

"'Be warned we smell fresh tourist meat,'" said Nils de Groot.

"*Dear*, your olfactory expertise is failing you," Nora de Groot said to her husband. "I smell lemongrass and jasmine."

"No, woman. Look!"

The rest of the tour group turned. Unlike its dismal interior, the clock tower's view was splendid. Pigeons darted and bobbed along the train tracks leading toward the wax factory; and in another direction, the tourists could make out the theater and the dairy. Below them, they saw the entire stretch of Florence Boulevard, which the mayor's team had closed off for that afternoon's parade. From that height, they caught only the barest glimpse inside the top-secret area, where something metallic reflected the sun. The highlight of the view was the town's seven quaint covered bridges, which usually had a friendly seven-word greeting spelled out across their roofs.

Today the bridges bore a different message.

"I *clearly* do not smell like meat. I'm wearing expensive cologne!" Blake Glide huffed.

"Who wrote that? How appalling...and vulgar... and revolting!" Mary Feemore exclaimed. The other members of the tour nodded vehemently.

Ellen smiled. No tourists, no Knightlorian. She was leading everyone back down the narrow staircase when Edgar spotted a figure hurrying toward the clock tower.

Stephanie Knightleigh had escaped from Mr. Hirschfeld while he was busy fixing the thermostat, but her short stint as museum custodian had left her even waxier. Although she had peeled some of the stuff from her skin, Edgar could see that her once-lilac dress was now aswirl with blue wax from the swimming pool, and her hair was completely caked. With every step, chunks fell from her clothing.

"We've got company, Sister," he said softly as Ellen exited the doorway.

"Quick, let's get them out of here and into the Black Tree Forest," Ellen said. "She'll never follow us in there."

"Who would dare?"

28. Forest March

The Black Tree Forest Preserve formed the southern and western borders of Nod's Limbs, reaching all the way up to the old wax factory. From the outside it looked like any other forest preserve, with towering pines and sweet, furry forest animals rustling about. But it wasn't called the Black Tree Forest for nothing. As one traveled deeper into the undergrowth, the forest became darker and murkier. The trees grew so tall and so thick and their branches stretched out so far that they twisted together to form a wooden ceiling, blocking out any hope of sunlight. Even on a cloudless day, a person out for a stroll in the woods could not see well enough to know where to step. Not many people went for walks in these woods, for fear of never finding their way out.

Except the twins. So much time spent in their house with its heavily curtained windows and burned-out lightbulbs left them comfortable with darkness. They explored the forest from time to time when they tired of playing inside their house or in the Gadget Graveyard. It was a great source for worms and caterpillars to hide in each other's beds. Yet, while they had tramped through much of the southern forest, whose edge lay just beyond Ricketts Road across from their house, the western edge was mostly unknown to them.

"This way, troop," Ellen said, gesturing with her Pet-pole at the preserve. Pet's eye gleamed when it saw where they were headed. It shifted on its perch.

"Excuse me," Mary Feemore interrupted, "I am sure we came from *that* direction. No more touring."

She pointed down Florence Boulevard, but didn't spot Stephanie Knightleigh marching toward them. Ellen did.

"Yes, that's right, but there is a *lovely* shortcut through the woods, and we know you must be tired," said Ellen. "We want to return you to your rooms as soon as possible." Blake Glide's face lit up at this promise of comfort and security. The de Groots were already moving toward the trees.

"The shortest route possible, please," muttered Nora.

The twins led them into the gloomy woods.

Not three minutes later, Stephanie reached the edge of the forest. She hesitated, scanning the first tier of vegetation. Then she drew a deep breath and plunged in.

29. Man-Eaters

"Is it just me or is it getting darker in here?" Blake Glide asked through clenched teeth.

"Don't tell me the big action hero is afraid of the dark," Alex Sai said.

"Don't be ridiculous," he replied, flinching as something snapped above their heads.

"What was that?" Mary Feemore asked, a slight tremble in her voice.

"A great variety of plant and animal life thrives in the Black Tree Forest," Ellen explained. "That is why the town made it a preserve a long time ago—to protect such rare animals as the man-eating sloth and the vampire bat."

"Bats? I hate bats!" Blake Glide shrieked, cowering against Alex Sai.

"Oh, you've got to be kidding me," she said, pushing him away. "Anyway, it's probably just Nod's missing limbs wandering around," she added with a laugh.

"Oh no! I totally forgot about him!" Blake Glide said.

The group continued groping through the forest.

"What are we doing here? There's not even a path," said Alex Sai, as a thin branch whipped back in her face.

"Shhh! You'll disturb the bats!" Blake Glide hissed.

"My shoes are shredding—I may require medical attention!" Nils de Groot said. "Someone call a podiatrist!"

"Something just touched my foot! SOMETHING

JUST TOUCHED MY FOOT!" Blake Glide yelled. The other tourists froze behind him.

"Never mind; it's okay. It was just my other foot."

Ellen spun around. "It's only a shortcut if we keep moving!"

Since Pet never really put up much of a fight, Ellen had not tied it very tightly to her rake. Thus, when she turned, the force of her motion propelled Pet forward, free of the ropes at last. It sailed off its perch, right onto the movie star's head.

"*Eeeek!* It's a man-eating sloth! IT'S GOT ME!" Blake Glide screamed.

He wrenched Pet off his head and tossed it away. Pet landed with a thud a couple of feet behind the tour group. Edgar dove for it, knocking Alex Sai into a patch of prickly ash.

The rest of the tourists stumbled blindly toward the light at the forest's edge, screeching along with Blake Glide.

Alex Sai wobbled as she stood. One of her high-heeled shoes had disappeared into the brush. "My favorite pair!" she wailed, limping along after the group and rubbing her scratches.

Unfortunately for Pet, Edgar managed to grab it before it could disappear among the trees. Ellen shook her head as she strapped it back onto her rake, tighter this time.

"Shame, shame, Pet," she said. "Where would you go in this forest anyway?" Pet blinked and seemed to bristle ever so slightly.

"Well, Brother," Ellen said, "this has been a most successful endeavor."

"Indeed, Sister," Edgar replied. "I think we can safely assume that none of these tourists will brag about their visit to Nod's Limbs anytime soon."

"Too bad for Knightleigh," said Ellen.

"And good for us. Long live the Gadget Grave-yard!" said Edgar.

"And Berenice!" Ellen added, and as they headed out of the forest, she and Edgar sang a song:

> *So it goes, our tourists' woes*
> *Turned them into Nod's Limbs' foes!*
> *They'd rather lose their pinkie toes*
> *Than come to town again.*
> *The Gadget Graveyard's choice debris*
> *Shall stand in perpetuity,*
> *And Knightleigh's plan will only be*
> *The inn that might have been.*

The twins followed far behind the tour group and congratulated each other on a job well done with thwacks on the back. Soon they could resume planning Operation: Whiplash.

30. A Smile in the Dark

Stephanie roamed deep into the woods. A low-hanging branch caught a waxy ringlet, and she stopped to untangle her hair and tighten her purple ribbons before forging ahead.

"Hello, tour group!" she called, tripping over a vine. "*Hello!* Where are you? It's Stephanie, your *real* tour guide!"

Thorny plants clutched at her, and she had only the sounds of skittering creatures and twittering birds for company. She reached a dense section of trees and called out again; it was nearly pitch-black.

Suddenly, a torrent of screams and running footsteps ripped through the darkness. Stephanie's breath caught in her throat; the noise seemed to be nearby, but she saw nothing until a flash of something white appeared in the distance.

"Tour group? Is that you over there?" She moved

unsteadily toward the flash but stopped short when she ran into one of the thick trees.

"Ow!" she cried.

She had stubbed her toe. Stephanie felt her way around the tree, and the twinkle of white appeared again. This time, however, it was mere inches from her face. She saw that it was a toothy smile and discovered that the tree was, well…not a tree.

"Aaaah! AAAAAAAH!" Stephanie ran screaming from the broad, glowing grin, back toward the distant sunlight.

At the edge of the forest, she stopped and looked behind her. No one was in sight. Not the smiling man, not the twins, not the tourists. She held her hand over her racing heart. Breathing hard, she stepped out into the street.

The VIPs stood a few yards away. They were a shivering island of bewilderment surrounded by great commotion, a storm of brass and drums and marching boots. The French Toast Festival Grand Parade had begun.

31. Grandstanding

Everyone loves a parade, but the good citizens of Nod's Limbs absolutely delighted in them. Mayor Knightleigh's popularity was due in part to his skill in the art of the Grand Parade, and his office sponsored them for such holidays as Friendly Senior Citizens Day, Providers of Computer Repair and Other Life-saving Services Day, and Take Your Briefcase to Work Day.

So it was no surprise that on this occasion, the Knightleigh administration was determined to create their finest spectacle yet. The French Toast Festival Parade was not merely grand, it was magnificent.

Nearly every business in town sponsored a flower-bedecked float. Magoo's Flowery had never been so busy filling orders, and by the morning of the festival, every flower in the store had been sold.

The Hearty Party shop ran out of streamers, balloons, and ribbons the day that Miss Croquet announced a bike-decorating contest and Mayor Knightleigh granted permission for all contestants to ride in the parade.

But parade days were most significant to the Nod's Limbs High School Marching Band, which rehearsed tirelessly in anticipation of strutting its stuff in public. At least, the younger marchers enjoyed the limelight; most of the seniors had permanent blisters from years of frequent performing.

The whole of Florence Boulevard was closed to traffic, and townspeople crowded the sidewalks. Rows of dancers dressed as pieces of toast linked their arms and kicked their way down the road, singing, and large syrup bottles strolled along waving to the masses. The band marched proudly behind them, playing the classic "Seventy-Six French Toasts Lead the Grand Parade." Next, with colorful swoops and swirls, came the Flag Corps and then a leaping battalion of baton twirlers.

Annie Krump and her best friend, Miles Knight-leigh, costumed as a pot of jam and a pat of butter, followed the twirlers. The two were thrilled to have such prominent roles in the parade, even if their outfits were a bit unwieldy. After them came a convertible bearing Mrs. French Toast, the woman whose recipe had won the cook-off. She wore a tiara made of rhinestone-studded forks and knives. Walking in for-mation behind the car were scout troops, athletic teams, and middle schoolers carrying hand-painted banners with messages like WE ♥ NOD'S LIMBS and NOD'S LIMBS ROCKS!

Next up were very large men on very small motorbikes, followed by the flower floats on which Nod's Limbs' oldest and youngest residents rode, throwing petals to well-wishers. Magoo's Flowery's float was just a bare wooden box on wheels with a hastily lettered sign that read "Magoo's Flowery Salutes the Community."

After the floats, winners of the Pretty Pet contests marched past. Donald Bogginer carried his cat Chauncey, whose mismatched eyes had won him first prize the previous year, but whose encounter with a python had since left him completely bald. The very end of the Grand Parade featured a color guard carrying the Nod's Limbs flag with solid swaths of the town colors, marigold and pea soup.

Meanwhile, up and down Florence Boulevard, volunteers distributed utensils to the onlookers.

"Forks and knives! Get your forks and knives here!" they yelled. "Can't eat your toast without a fork!"

This spectacle greeted the tourists when they emerged, screaming, from the Black Tree Forest Preserve.

32. Swept Away

The townspeople caught sight of their celebrated guests and whooped and cheered and clapped even louder than before. The passing trumpeters trilled their horns, and their brassy tones sounded above the other noise. Those people nearest the VIPs surged toward them, bombarding them with pleasantries.

"Enjoy your tour?"

"Wasn't the Museum of Wax charming? My little Bertie is featured there! And Miss Croquet—such a lovely teacher!"

"Barbarino has the best sandwiches, eh? Nod's Limbs' finest!"

"How about the view from that clock tower?"

The tourists huddled close together. An elderly woman dressed as a syrup bottle shouted something incoherent at Blake Glide.

Alex Sai was the first to spot the fork clutched in the woman's bony hand.

"What are these lunatics doing?" she asked. "They're all armed!"

"Where are our guides? They've abandoned us!" whimpered Nora de Groot. "Take me home, Nils, I want to go *home*!"

"I don't like the way they're waving that cutlery," her husband replied. "And why are they staring at us like that?"

"Heaven help us!" shrieked Blake Glide. "'Fresh tourist meat'—they're going to eat us!"

Mary Feemore squeaked and grabbed Blake Glide's arm. "Look!" she cried.

Stephanie Knightleigh had spotted them.

"At last I've got you!" she shouted above the din. "Come with me—I'll take you where you need to go!"

But the visitors did not recognize the well-groomed girl who had stood outside the Hotel Motel holding a plate of croissants. Instead, they saw the contagious student who tried to attack them at the Museum of Wax. She looked more menacing than ever, covered as she was with twigs and leaves and bellowing hysterically.

Alex Sai spoke just loudly enough for the other tourists to hear her.

"If we all act calm, we just might make it out of this French toast thing alive," she said. "Nobody panic."

"That's right! Nobody pancake! I mean, *panic*!" shouted Blake Glide.

He started pushing his way through a throng of knife-and-fork-carrying autograph seekers.

"Yes!" the mob cried. "Yes, into the parade! Our guests of honor should be in the parade!" The tide of people propelled the VIPs into the middle of the high school band. Powerless to resist, the tourists were swept along the road like driftwood.

"Where are our tour guides?" wailed Nora de Groot again, but her cry was lost in the crush of excitement around her.

33. Victory Nigh

In fact, the tour guides had just come out of the forest and stood by the road, taking in the scene.

"What a disgusting display," said Edgar.

"They're dressed like *toast*," said Ellen, leaning on her Pet-pole. "I wonder how our tourists are doing? Come on, I want to be there when they tell Knight-leigh what a terrible place Nod's Limbs is."

As they wove through the crowd, they passed Stephanie who, for the third time that day, had lost her tour. When she saw the twins, her top lip curled and her eyes narrowed.

"Stephanie, you look terrible," Edgar called. "Long day?"

"You don't have to worry about your celebrities," added Ellen. "I think Nod's Limbs has made a lasting impression on them!"

"Ooooooooooo—*hellions!*"

Stephanie reached for Ellen's throat, but the twins slipped away like eels. Stephanie tried to push after them, but a lifetime of wriggling through tight passages and trapdoors gave Edgar and Ellen the advantage. They quickly lost her in the procession snaking its way toward Town Hall.

34. Speechifying

Citizens, band members, baton twirlers, tourists, and very large men (having parked their very small motorbikes) flowed into the grassy area in front of Town Hall. Mayor Knightleigh stood behind a microphone on the front steps. He clapped his hands when he saw his VIPs.

The crowd quieted and the visitors clung to one another, sensitive to any sudden movements from the apparently hungry masses. Feedback squealed from the microphone, and the mayor's voice blared forth:

> *"Ladies and gentlemen, my fellow Nod's Limbsians! Welcome to the First Annual French Toast Festival!"*

The horde cheered and banged their forks and knives together. The tourists shuddered.

> *"In just a moment, I shall unveil my Top Secret Surprise! But first I want to thank our distinguished guests for gracing us with their distinguished presences. As sophisticated consumers of tourism opportunities the world over, you will surely agree that Nod's Limbs deserves a place in the National Registry of Historic Treasures!*
>
> *"By now, you have seen all that Nod's Limbs has to offer, and I know in my heart that your thorough enjoyment of today's tour—given by the finest of Nod's Limbs' youth—will linger with you for the rest of your lives. It is our honor to have you for dinner this evening!"*

At the word *dinner,* Blake Glide's eyes rolled back in his head, and he fainted against the de Groots.

Another clash of cutlery, and a woman yelled out, "I brought my own powdered sugar!" She tossed a handful of the confection into the air, and the sweet confetti blew through the spectators. Children jumped up to catch the sugar on their tongues like snowflakes.

35. Behind the Curtain

All the while, Edgar and Ellen hid behind some toast-clad revelers near the front of the crowd, relishing the frightened faces of the visitors and, in particular, Blake Glide's fainting spell. Then they noticed the enormous curtain just to the left of Town Hall where, mere hours ago, the barricade had stood.

While the mayor droned on, the twins slipped off to take a peek.

Edgar and Ellen passed beneath the curtain and Edgar instinctively grabbed Ellen's pigtail.

Lo! Before them stood a colossal piece of French toast, lustrous and golden and slightly browner at the crusts. Next to it was an enormous pitcher made of bolted metal plates, at least two stories tall, and labeled MAPLE SYRUP.

"That is one big piece of toast," said Ellen. Her stomach growled.

Eyeing the syrup, Edgar removed Heimertz's wrench from his satchel and held it to his heart.

"A mess of which I have only dreamed," he murmured and stepped up to the nearest bolt.

To build the pitcher, the mayor had hired a special squad of kitchenware designers. A construction team had spent the whole week behind the barricade on ladders, cranes, and scaffolds, bolting together huge sheets of steel and rigging a complex pulley system that would allow the mayor to pour the topping onto the toast.

Edgar went to work removing the bolts one by one. Wherever he pulled one out with the wrench, a thick dribble of syrup escaped down the pitcher's side.

"Here, make yourself useful," Edgar said, tossing his sister one of the ropes hanging from the lip of the pitcher. Ellen pulled it taut, and Edgar climbed up, removing bolts as he went.

With her back to the curtain, Ellen didn't see a wax-encrusted head appear beneath the heavy drape.

"You," growled Stephanie Knightleigh. "You monsters have ruined everything."

She lunged at Ellen, who dropped the rope, deflected Stephanie's grasp with her Pet-pole, and ran behind the pitcher. Edgar swung helplessly above, smacking into the metal wall again and again.

"OW!" he yelped, banging his elbow.

The mayor's daughter stalked the perimeter of the giant pitcher.

"I saw the two of you sneak in here. You think you're *soooo* tricky, don't you?"

She brushed against the metal sheeting and felt something gluey.

"Oh, *now* look what you've done," she cried, examining the holes in the pitcher. "Are you cretins trying to destroy the whole festival?"

"Bolt by sticky-sweet bolt," Ellen declared, popping up behind the giant piece of toast.

Stephanie chased Ellen and tackled her. Edgar, hanging high above them, cried out, "Hey, I'm the only one who gets to clobber Ellen!"

36. Sticky Fingers

The girls' noisy brawl did not go unheard. Edgar saw the velvet curtain shake, and a short, squat pat of butter stumbled through.

"What's going on back here?" asked Miles Knightleigh. His freckled face stuck out of a hole in the center of his costume.

"*Psst*... Help! Help!" Edgar called down. Stephanie was throttling Ellen out of sight behind the huge piece of French toast.

Miles looked up and saw a boy in striped pajamas dangling from the lip of the pitcher.

"What's wrong?" he asked.

"It's Stephanie! She's fallen into the syrup and can't get out!"

"Oh no!" Miles said.

"I can't save her!" Edgar cried. "It's up to you— your suit will float!"

"I'll do my best!" Miles spotted a ladder leaning against the pitcher that led all the way to its top. Waddling over in his awkward costume, he shouted, "I'm coming, Stephie!"

He started climbing.

"Please hurry! Every second counts!" Edgar called after him.

Once sure that Miles was on his way up, Edgar strained over the edge of the toast to see how Ellen was doing. Stephanie had her by the pigtails and was pushing her face into the crust.

"You get the first bite!" she screeched. Ellen blindly swung her Pet-pole about, entirely missing her opponent.

"Excuse me, Stephanie," Edgar yelled down. "Isn't that your brother up there? He looks like he might get into some awful trouble." He swung out a spindly leg and pointed a footie toward the ladder.

"Oh my gosh!" exclaimed Stephanie. "Miles! *What are you doing?*"

Miles was concentrating hard and didn't hear his sister's cries. Although Stephanie quickly reached the ladder, Miles was already at the top, standing at the lip of the syrup vat. He looked down into the shiny liquid, but sunlight reflected too brightly off the surface to see anything.

Holding his nose, Miles placed one foot against the edge of the pitcher and jumped.

What a very brave butter pat.

37. The Big Book of Universal Records

Unaware of the drama unfolding behind the curtain, Mayor Knightleigh was recapping the day's events, congratulating Mrs. French Toast, and smiling down at the quivering VIPs.

But the townspeople were growing restless.

"What's behind that curtain?" they began to shout.

The mayor raised his hands to calm the crowd. A flick of his pudgy fingers brought a small group of people to the steps, each clad in a yellow rubber suit and paper face mask.

"Narshampians!" cried Blake Glide. He nearly fainted a second time, but Nils de Groot slapped him awake.

> *"These gentlemen are from the* Big Book of Universal Records. *I invited them here today to document Nod's Limbs' soon-to-be record-breaking triumph, the crowning achievement of any French Toast Festival. I give you...the largest piece of French toast ever in the history of the universe!"*

With another flourish of trumpets, the curtain dropped to reveal the toast. People oohed and even the tourists perked up a bit.

> *"Now, I ask the verification team to measure our magnificent and record-setting feat, and after that, I say — 'Let them eat toast!'"*

Knightleigh closed his eyes and leaned back proudly, waiting for the deafening applause.

None came.

The mayor opened one eye and saw his spectators gawking at the syrup pitcher, on which a mottled girl waved and yelled while a pajama-clad boy dangled on a rope from its lip.

"Who is that girl?" asked Mary Feemore.

"It looks like...like...," said Nils de Groot.

"PRUNELLA CRUDLEY!" screamed Blake Glide.

"She's after our poor tour assistant! Oh, look at him hanging there," wailed Nora de Groot, "like a pathetic worm on a fishhook."

"Some bodyguard," muttered Alex Sai.

Mayor Knightleigh peered at the pitcher.

"Stephanie!"

38. Gone Swimming

Stephanie leaned over the lip of the pitcher, trying to grab hold of her brother's costume as he flailed about.

"Stephanie! What in the name of Nod is going on?" the mayor yelled.

"Nothing, Daddy," she said through gritted teeth. "Everything's under control. Miles, quick, give me your hand."

"Get down from there right this minute, young lady, or there will be no…er…no French toast for you!"

Suddenly, the crowd heard a loud, creaking groan, and the giant pitcher shuddered. Stephanie wobbled and nearly lost her balance.

Now, if one wanted to eat the Universe's Largest Piece of French Toast, one would need a lot of maple syrup to go with it. After careful calculation, the mayor's engineers had concluded that they needed the equivalent of 513,080 bottles of syrup to smother the piece of toast adequately. Something the size of a dump truck was not big enough to hold it all. Even something the size of a cement mixer was not big enough. So Knightleigh commissioned a pitcher that held as much liquid as a swimming pool. Thus, 513,080 bottles worth of pure maple syrup pressed against the walls of the pitcher, now weakened by Edgar and his wrench.

And as Miles continued to thrash about, and Stephanie continued to reach for him, and Edgar continued to dangle from the rope, the pitcher let out one last low, metallic moan.

39. Smells Like Syrup

Ker-klang!

Without enough bolts to hold them in place, the steel plates buckled and separated. The pitcher ruptured with thunderous force, and a cascade of goo gushed onto the toast and the people below.

Stephanie just managed to grab a corner of Miles's costume, and as the syrup poured forth, so too did the butter pat, with his sister along for her second swim of the day.

"Wheeeeeee!" clamored Miles as he rode the wave.

"Whyyyyy meeeeee?" shrieked Stephanie as the torrent swept her along.

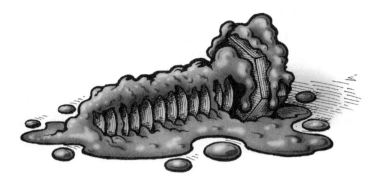

Too late, the spectators tried to run. They could do nothing as sticky ooze flowed everywhere, smacking against ankles and shins. Those who turned to flee lost their footing and fell into the rising pond, pulling their neighbors down with them.

Edgar plummeted onto the toast in a tangle of pulleys and ropes. Ellen lay just a few feet away where Stephanie had left her in the swollen bread. The twins greedily licked their lips and fingers, and then looked out over the audience.

No one could move; every face was full of shock and syrup. The floats had been splashed, and gooey posies and daisies sank into the chicken wire that had held them aloft. The high school band members looked on helplessly as liquid ran out of trumpet bells and trombone slides. Batons stuck to their twirlers' hands, and Nancy Weedle's sheepdog, Dudley, was indistinguishable from Mrs. Jackson's basset hound, Roxy.

But the tourists had gotten the worst of it. In their place of honor, they were nearest the French toast when the pitcher burst. The syrup was like sweet cement, gluing them to the ground and to each other.

Stephanie landed on her father, but fortunately for her, his large belly broke her fall.

Nearby, a butter pat floundered.

"Dad?" said Miles. "I'm stuck."

40. Measure for Measure

Grunts and groans filled the air as the good citizens of Nod's Limbs tried to break free of their maple prison.

Edgar and Ellen, meanwhile, were having a difficult time getting off the French toast—it was very thick, and, now, soft and mushy. With every step, their scrawny legs disappeared into the sponginess. Finally, they dropped off the edge and hid behind a large planter on the town hall steps.

From there they spied their tour group trying to separate themselves from one another, though long gooey strands still joined them. The twins watched Blake Glide drag his sticky fingers through his stickier hair and Alex Sai rub at her speckled sunglasses.

"I'd better call my agent," moaned the actor. "These lunatics aren't capable of appreciating serious dinner theater."

Nils de Groot wiped syrup from his forehead and tried to free his precious shoes. "We should have known this visit would be wretched, Nora. Wind chimes don't lie."

Mayor Knightleigh trudged back to his microphone and looked out over his stunned constituents. He tried to salvage the situation:

> *"My fellow citizens! People! This is but a minor setback. We still have the Universe's Largest Piece of French Toast! Let us not forget why we gathered here to celebrate. Gentlemen, let the measurement commence!"*

Mayor Knightleigh, applauding, turned to his rubber-protected verification team.

One of the yellow-suited figures removed his face mask. "Sorry, Mr. Mayor. We can't measure your French toast. It has absorbed a considerable amount of syrup, so its mass has expanded.

"Your entry into the Breads and Starches subsection of the Universe's Largest Food category is hereby disqualified."

The other face masks nodded.

The crowd groaned.

Edgar and Ellen grinned.

The mayor snapped.

"What do you mean 'disqualified'?" he shrieked. "My hard-earned accomplishment! My well-deserved honor! You will go over and measure that toast *right this instant!*"

The team from the *Big Book of Universal Records* shook their heads.

Knightleigh stomped his feet and kicked the lectern. He wrenched the microphone off its stand and flung it into the audience. When an aide tried to calm him, the mayor nearly threw him down the steps. Finally, he just sank to his knees and buried his face in his hands.

41. A Mayoral Setback

After a few moments, Mary Feemore approached the mayor.

"Mayor Knightleigh?" she said.

"It's all ruined," he moaned, dismissing her.

"Mr. Mayor, I—"

"Now Nod's Limbs will never be on the map. We'll never see another tourist!"

"My name is Mary Feemore."

"That's nice," he said, looking over her shoulder.

She continued. "I'm not actually a writer for a travel brochure company."

"Oh, that's too bad."

"I'm an inspector for the National Registry of Historic Treasures."

Now the mayor looked directly at Mary Feemore. "Huh? You're a what? But the brochures...?" he sputtered.

"I was sent to do a secret evaluation of Nod's Limbs' application for National Registry status, and I just wanted to let you know that when I'm done with my report, your town will certainly be on the map, sir...."

"Yes?" Mayor Knightleigh's eyes brightened.

"As an unsafe locality!" she continued, looking down at her syrup-drenched shoes and scratched arms. "I'm forwarding this case to the Federal Inquiry Board for acts of a suspicious nature. As far as I'm concerned, your whole town belongs in a mental institution."

Mayor Knightleigh shook his head. "No! This was my day! All my plans! My hard work! Oh, *why me?*"

As he fumbled in front of Mary Feemore, the

once-bright afternoon sky darkened, and a black cloud spread across the horizon.

"Oh, great," said Alex Sai. "That's all we need to end this endless day—rain."

42. It's All for the Birds

Not even Edgar and Ellen could have planned what happened next. A dark cloud did indeed roll over Town Hall, but it was not a rain cloud.

It was a pigeon cloud.

Now, pigeons spend most of their lives clucking, cooing, waddling around, and generally getting in people's way. They are, by and large, hungry birds and beggars to boot, and they think that being underfoot will cause passersby to drop them a bread crumb or two, or maybe even a candy bar. But they rarely get more than crumbs, because passersby tend to want to eat their own candy bars, so pigeons continue clucking and cooing and waddling and begging.

But pigeons are also greedy birds, and when a feast the size of the Universe's Largest Piece of French Toast appears, they stop begging and they *take.*

A great mass of pigeons hovered above Town Hall, casting a shadow on the people gathered below; those who looked up had only a moment to prepare themselves for the onslaught. One bird, and then another, and soon hundreds plunged into the mess of people and instruments and pets. The birds were not particular where they dove. The glistening syrup coating both toast and crowd attracted them like a beacon.

Pandemonium!

The first wave of birds swooped in on the deepest pool of syrup at the base of Town Hall's front steps. One pigeon landed on Mary Feemore's head and stuck in her hair. Blake Glide, remembering his recent brush with carnivores in the forest, shielded his own coif and yelled to Alex Sai, "More man-eaters! Better get down!" He dropped to the ground and lay facedown in a gummy puddle.

Nils de Groot batted at the winged tormentors. Sadly, he misjudged every pigeon's trajectory and speed and failed to make contact with a single one. His wife wisely scuttled under an abandoned tuba for shelter.

Alex Sai neither screamed nor fled. Instead, she sat quiet and motionless in the chaos, and was thus largely ignored by the flying flock.

Beyond the tour group, birds pecked the flag corps' glittery uniforms. They swarmed over the marching band's instruments, the syrup-coated syrup bottle costumes, and the French toast–clad dancers.

Alex Sai took in the spectacle, her lost shoe, the blob she could not wipe off her expensive sunglasses, and this bizarre little town she had been so loathe to visit. Then she laughed, loudly and heartily.

She laughed so hard she doubled over, so hard her sides hurt and tears streamed down her face. She removed her one shoe, tossed it aside, and slid barefoot out of the pigeon blitz.

43. Have Your Toast and Eat It Too

Meanwhile, most of the birds had found the main course: the gigantic piece of French toast. Once a moist, golden breakfast treat, the toast was now a feathery, gray mass, and despite the immensity of the syrup-inflated bread, the horde of pigeons was even larger. And very, very hungry. Soon nothing but crumbs remained of the piece of French toast that had once been, unofficially, the universe's largest.

Stephanie Knightleigh hunched near the town hall steps, trying to help Miles to his feet. The butter pat—now dripping with sugary goodness—was an inviting target, and he and Stephanie found themselves at the center of a feeding frenzy. Sometimes instead of a gooey treat, the pigeons got a beak full of waxy dress or, more painfully, fleshy earlobe. Miles's costume protected him from most of the pecking and scratching, but Stephanie was at the birds' mercy.

"I...HATE...THOSE...TWINS!" she yelled, but clucking and f luttering drowned out her voice. "Daddy—OUCH!"

Edgar and Ellen danced out from behind the planter.

"You really *shouldn't* feed the pigeons, Stephanie," Ellen called, shaking her Pet-pole disapprovingly. "They'll just follow you around forever."

Edgar scanned the extensive mess they had caused.

"Come on. The show is over," he said. "Let's go."

"What a day we've had. Knightleigh's plan is a total failure! There's no way anybody will visit Nod's Limbs ever again."

"No need for hotel rooms if you don't have guests to fill them. The Gadget Graveyard is safe!" said Edgar.

"So is Berenice," said Ellen. "Mission accomplished." The two whacked each other happily.

And because every dark pigeon cloud has a silver lining, the twins sang a little victory ditty on their way home. Ellen swung her rake back and forth in time to their music.

> *Beyond the plots where dead men dwell,*
> *We'll dance upon the gadget swell—*
> *Here's to the junk that serves us well!*
> *And down with Knightleigh's new hotel!*
> *It's better than we could expect—*
> *Syrup-covered, pigeon-pecked,*
> *And Knightleigh never did suspect*
> *The terror that we could inject.*
> *What laughs, what fun, what tours we run!*
> *What pranking! Now our battle's won!*

44. Chills and Spills

As afternoon deepened into dusk, Edgar and Ellen teetered atop tall piles of junk, drinking in the view of their Gadget Graveyard.

"Doesn't it seem *extra* magnificent today?" said Edgar.

"Everything is right where it belongs—and every-thing will stay right where it belongs," said Ellen.

With contented sighs, the two skipped down the piles and set off to find Berenice.

Ellen fed her and, just because she was so happy, she let Berenice nibble her big toe.

"So, Brother, what are we going to do tomorrow?"

"Operation: Whiplash, of course," he answered.

He pulled out the wrench and went to work removing an old wardrobe door from its hinges.

Ellen picked up Pet, still tied to its rake. "That can wait, Edgar," she said. "For now, a toast." She held out the Pet-pole. "To *toast!*"

"And to pigeons!" cried Edgar, clinking wrench against rake.

The sun had not yet set, but a shadow spilled over them. From the chill in their bones, the twins knew whose shadow it was; they slowly turned to face Heimertz.

The caretaker loomed, smiling his mad, eerie smile. Ellen gulped. Edgar blinked. Neither made a sound. With a sudden jerk, he grabbed his wrench from Edgar with one hand, and with the other he snatched Pet away from Ellen. Silently, he put the

Pet-pole over his shoulder, pivoted on his heel, and lumbered away.

In the quiet of the Gadget Graveyard, the twins looked at each other, too unnerved to speak.

It was then that they heard a sound like an approaching roll of thunder. And it was coming closer.

Having concluded their feast, the pigeons were heading back to their nests, their bloated little bird tummies full of toast and syrup. And, as birds do, they had to rid themselves of their meal to make room for the next one. To the twins' horror, their beloved Gadget Graveyard was directly in the pigeons' flight path.

It started slowly.

Plop!

Plop! Plop!

And then it rained.

Plop! Plop! Plop! Plop!

"*Eeeeeeeeeeeee!*" Edgar and Ellen ran shrieking toward their house. For the first time in many months, baths seemed imminent.

THE END

Nod's Limbs: What a Trip!

by Alex Sai

Capital Times Chief Travel Editor

EVERY ONCE IN AWHILE, one comes upon a small town that is so boring, undistinguished, and dreary that one hopes for bad weather just to have something to talk about.

Nod's Limbs is not that kind of town.

Nod's Limbs is edgy, exotic, and full of surprises. It's as vital and crazy as the Village in the sixties (not that I was there), and a visitor never has a moment's rest. If you're looking for a relaxing spa getaway of beaches, poolside fruit infusions, and quantum yoga, Nod's Limbs is not for you. Visiting this place is more like being whipped with oak leaves at a Turkish bath.

Great fun and terrific sightseeing exists around every corner. For your first trip, a long weekend will suffice to get a feel for the place and take in some of the quirkier features.

Start day one by taking an easy stroll through the lovely residential area, where normal-looking small-town residents interacting in typical small-town ways belie their "alien" origin. Yes, they say they're from the planet Narshamp! Keep your eyes peeled for extraterrestrial shrub artistry.

Make a brief stop at the clock tower, where you can't beat the view of the quaintly funky covered bridges. Take time to examine what remains of the town's lengthy tradition of public executions.

Bloodstains that have stood the test of time create an especially vivid atmosphere.

The spooky landmark perfectly prepares you for your first meal in Nod's Limbs at the local Italian restaurant, where the proprietor himself, Mr. Barbarino, will prepare your lunch. He serves little-known northern Italian specialties that tickle the adventuresome eater.

A walk through the nearby park offers a chance to digest, as well as a look at a strange work of art: the limbless statue of the town's founder.

Further activities for the afternoon and subsequent days include the fantastic Nod's Limbs Museum of Wax, which is both waxy and wacky; the municipal beach (watch out for the quicksand!); and the famed Crabby Apple Tree, whose branches provide shelter for the weary and the wicked.

If you can get a reservation on the local government's official tour, it's worth planning ahead: the youthful tour guides are informative and willing to go "off-road" for an interested group.

You might also try coordinating your trip around one of their many festivals. The French Toast Festival is a favorite, but it's clear that you never know what will happen at any of them.

Don't be surprised if the citizens of Nod's Limbs wave, shout compliments, or even hold a parade in your honor. The community, at its essence, is a celebration of folk traditions and rustic culture, and it welcomes visitors with an offbeat but warm embrace.

As for accommodations, for now there's just one game in town: the Hotel Motel. But plans are afoot for a new luxury hotel, so make your reservations early. Rumor has it that the International Breakfast Foods Association is considering making Nod's Limbs the site of their annual conference.

Edgar & Ellen

UNDER TOWN

SOMEONE IS CAUSING a lot of trouble in the charming town of Nod's Limbs, but it isn't Edgar and Ellen! To catch this new mischievous miscreant and end the rash of copycat capers, the twins must scour the sewers and uncover someone's dirty secret.

BOOK 3 OF THE EDGAR & ELLEN SERIES
Coming Soon!

WWW.EDGARANDELLEN.COM

READ ON FOR A SNEAK PREVIEW OF THE TERRIBLE TWINS' NEXT ADVENTURE.

Morning Breaks

The rising sun lingered behind the eastern hills of Nod's Limbs, reluctant, perhaps, to show its face on such a crisp morning. Municipal street sweepers Claudius Roe and his son Charlie neared the end of their morning rounds and paused at the foot of a driveway. Leaning on his broom, Claudius read the front-page headline of the day's *Gazette*:

KNIGHTLORIAN HOTEL CONSTRUCTION TO BEGIN

Smelterburg Construction Corporation Racing to Meet Foundation Day Deadline

"So, they're building that hotel after all. It's a miracle considering the French Toast Festival disaster—all those traumatized celebrities," he said.

"That journalist gal didn't seem to mind," said Charlie. "Thanks to her article on our town, the mayor gets to build his hotel, and we get tourists to sweep up after—"

His father jerked his head around.

"Pop? Hey, Pop, are you okay?"

Twigs snapped and a low snarl rose from the cemetery across the street. Charlie could see faint outlines of gravestones, row upon row, solemn and still in the dim morning light. The sound persisted as something flitted among the stone markers and disappeared.

The snarl stopped and all was silent.

"Uh, Pop? It, uh…it's almost dawn…. Maybe we'd better, uh…move along…."

Charlie turned to see his father swiftly walking away.

"When you're right, you're right," Claudius called back.

As the two men hurried off, a hooded figure passed from the cemetery into the neighboring junkyard, stopping to gaze at a very tall, very narrow house. One light shone through a round window on a top floor; the rest lay in darkness.

A hand reached into the folds of a cloak and withdrew a dingy photograph. It revealed a bizarre scene of dozens of terrified people, coated in goop and shrinking in terror beneath a cloud of attacking birds. In the background, however, there were two figures dressed in striped footie pajamas who did not cower. They looked nearly identical but that one was a girl and the other a boy. In the midst of chaos, they appeared to be dancing.

The figure crumpled the photograph, stashed it inside the cloak, then vanished into the mist.

Read where the mischief begins...

Edgar & Ellen

RARE BEASTS

EDGAR AND ELLEN DREAM BIG when it comes to pranks. After they hear that exotic animals are worth tons of money, the twins come up with the ultimate get-rich-quick scheme that sends Nod's Limbs into a frenzy. Alas for the devilish duo, strange creatures like Mondopillars and Hambles do not always get along....

Rare Beasts
BOOK 1 OF THE EDGAR & ELLEN SERIES
Available Now at Your Favorite Bookseller

Edgar & Ellen

PET'S REVENGE

WHOSE LAB HAVE the twins discovered? What are the secrets of the old journal? And what has gotten into Pet? The mystery deepens as Pet fights back.

BOOK 4 OF THE EDGAR & ELLEN SERIES
Coming Soon!

WWW.EDGARANDELLEN.COM

Enjoy Edgar & Ellen?
Add to the adventure at
www.edgarandellen.com!

ENTER THE WONDERFULLY WICKED WORLD OF
EDGAR & ELLEN! Become a reporter for the
Nod's Limbs Gazette and use your byline to share
the horrible truth!
Write your own
mischievous tales star-
ing Edgar & Ellen!
Watch the cartoon
or play the
diabolically
great games!

EXPERIENCE
www.edgarandellen.com

Use this code to access top-secret areas of the site: UD2A4E1R5G3S

Edgar & Ellen®

MISCHIEF & MAYHEM™ GAME

Play pranks and wreak havoc around Nod's Limbs in this darkly humorous board game.

G9136

H2257

GLOW-IN-THE-DARK PUZZLE

Piece together Edgar & Ellen's latest misadventure. Their gadgets glow!

TELL US IN 100 WORDS OR LESS WHERE YOU THINK PET COMES FROM . . . AND BE ENTERED FOR A CHANCE TO WIN A FREE DIGITAL VIDEO CAMERA TO KEEP THOSE CREATIVE IDEAS COMING!

Edgar & Ellen Video Camera Sweepstakes

Official Rules

NO PURCHASE NECESSARY.

To enter the Edgar & Ellen Video Camera Sweepstakes write your name, telephone number, and full mailing address on a 3" x 5" card, and tell us in 100 words or less where you think Pet (Edgar and Ellen's hairy, one-eyed pet) comes from. Mail the card, in a stamped envelope, to: Edgar & Ellen Video Camera Sweepstakes, Simon & Schuster Children's Publishing Division, Marketing Department, 1230 Avenue of the Americas, 4th floor, New York, New York 10020. Limit one (1) entry per person. Limit one (1) prize per household. Not responsible for: postage due, late, lost, stolen, damaged, not delivered, mutilated, illegible, or misdirected entries, or for typographical errors in the rules. Entries void if they are in whole or in part illegible, incomplete, or damaged. Sweepstakes starts January 1, 2006. All entries must be postmarked by March 25, 2006, and received by March 31, 2006.

All entries become the property of Sponsor and will not be acknowledged or returned. By submitting an entry, all entrants grant Sponsor the absolute and unconditional right and authority to copy, edit, publish, promote, broadcast, or otherwise use, in whole or in part, their entries, in perpetuity, in any manner without further permission, notice, or compensation.

Simon & Schuster Inc. ("Sponsor") will award one (1) grand prize, one (1) second prize, and one (1) third prize to be chosen by a Sponsor representative from a random drawing of all eligible entries received. Grand prize includes the following: one digital video camera, one Edgar & Ellen Mischief & Mayhem game from Mattel, one Edgar & Ellen 250-piece glow-in-the-dark poster puzzle from Mattel, and one set of four Edgar & Ellen books signed by the author/illustrator. Total approximate retail value of grand prize: $400.00. Second prize includes the following: one Edgar & Ellen Mischief & Mayhem game from Mattel, one Edgar & Ellen 250-piece glow-in-the-dark poster puzzle from Mattel, and one set of four Edgar & Ellen books signed by the author/illustrator. Total approximate retail value of second prize: $75.00. Third prize includes one set of four Edgar & Ellen books signed by the author/illustrator. Total approximate retail value of third prize: $40.00. Total retail value of all prizes to be awarded: $515.00. The three prize winners will be selected at random from all eligible entries received in a drawing to be held on or about April 15, 2006. Winners will be notified by mail and telephone within thirty days of selection. If any prize or prize notification is returned as undeliverable, if any winner rejects his/her prize, or in the event of a winner's noncompliance with these sweepstakes rules and requirements, such prize will be forfeited and an alternate winner will be selected from all remaining eligible entries. Upon prize forfeiture, no compensation will be given. Odds of winning depend on the number of eligible entries received. Any entries deemed inappropriate for any reason will be disqualified, at the Sponsor's sole discretion.

Sweepstakes is open to legal residents of the continental U.S. (excluding Puerto Rico) and Canada (except Quebec), ages 7-14 as of January 1, 2006. Proof of age is required to claim prize. Prizes will be delivered to and awarded in the name of the winner's parent or legal guardian. Void in Puerto Rico, Quebec, and wherever prohibited or restricted by law. All provincial, federal, state, and local laws apply. Employees of Sponsor, Simon & Schuster Canada, and their respective suppliers, parent companies, subsidiaries, affiliates, agencies, and participating retailers, and persons connected with the use, marketing, or conducting of this sweepstakes, are not eligible. Family members living in the same household as any of the individuals referred to in the preceding sentence are not eligible.

Prizes are not transferable, have no cash equivalent, and may not be substituted except by Sponsor, in the event of prize unavailability, in which case a prize of equal or greater value will be awarded.

If the winner is a Canadian resident, then he/she must correctly answer a skill-based question administered by mail.

All expenses on receipt and use of prizes including provincial, federal, state, and local taxes are the sole responsibility of the of the winner's parent or legal guardian. Winner's parent or legal guardian will be required to execute and return on winners' behalf an Affidavit of Eligibility and a Liability/Publicity Release and all other legal documents which the sweepstakes Sponsor may require (including a W-9 tax form) within fifteen days of attempted notification or an alternate winner may be selected.

By accepting a prize, winner grants to Sponsor the right to use his/her name and likeness for any advertising, promotion, and publicity purposes without further compensation or permission, except where prohibited by law.

By participating in the sweepstakes, entrants agree to be bound by these rules and the decisions of the judges and Sponsor, which are final in all matters relating to this sweepstakes. Failure to comply with these official rules may result in disqualification of your entry and prohibition of any further participation in this sweepstakes.

By entering, entrants release Sponsor and its subsidiaries, affiliates, divisions, advertising, production, and promotion agencies from any and all liability for any loss, harm, damages, costs, or expenses, including without limitation property damages, personal injury, and/or death, arising out of participation in this sweepstakes, the acceptance, possession, use or misuse of any prize, claims based on publicity rights, rights of privacy, intellectual property rights, copyright infringement, defamation, or merchandise delivery.

For the first names and states of residence of the prize winners (available after April 30, 2006), send a separate, stamped, self-addressed envelope to: Winners List, Edgar & Ellen Video Camera Sweepstakes, Simon & Schuster Children's Marketing Department, 1230 Avenue of the Americas, New York, New York 10020. All prize winners list requests must be received by May 30, 2006

Sponsor: Simon & Schuster Children's Publishing, 1230 Avenue of the Americas, New York, NY 10020.

Aladdin Paperbacks
Simon & Schuster Children's Publishing Division
www.SimonSaysKids.com

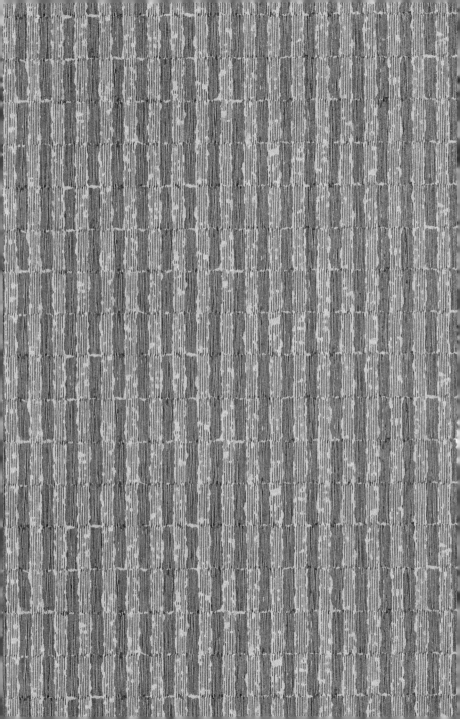